TO HAVE AND TO HOLD

RETURNING HOME BOOK 3

SERENA BELL

JELSBA
MEDIA
GROUP

PROLOGUE

Hunter Cross made Trina Levine laugh at the most inopportune moment, and her orgasm, which had been building for what felt like hours, broke up and drifted apart the way the colors of the clouds do once the sun has dipped below the horizon. But she didn't care, because it was so good to laugh with him, so good to be with him, lying on a blanket on a soft bed of pine needles in the woods.

"I've never done it outside before," she confessed, her cheek secure in the dip between the cap of his shoulder and the hard curve of his pec, a space just for her. Both of them were breathing hard, and his face, when she snuck a look at it, was as relaxed as she'd ever seen it, a soft, secret smile tugging up the corners of his mouth.

His arms tightened around her. "Me neither."

She could have said so many other things. *I've never laughed like this before. I've never come like this before. I've never felt like this before.* But she held back the words—even though she hadn't held back, not even a little, during their lovemaking. Because it was the night before he was going to leave and because she didn't know for sure yet if he felt the same way, and because it seemed like a lot to put on an evening that was already so full.

It had been the best kind of comedy of errors. They had each wanted to surprise the other, so both—without consulting—had hired babysitters, bought flowers, made dinner reservations.

Booked a hotel room.

Great minds think alike, Hunter had said, when the redundancy had come to light.

And in the end, two sets of hotel reservations had gone unused because a hotel room was too small for what they were feeling. Instead, they'd hiked to a spot he knew, a secret spot, and here they were.

"Trina."

Her heart, which was still pounding from the sustained intensity of their lovemaking, from the shock and power of her orgasm, from laughter, sped up. He sounded so—serious.

"I've fallen in love with you."

A wave of warmth and happiness swept over her. She'd been thinking the same thing for days, the words wanting to burst out at all kinds of crazy moments. Making dinner together in his kitchen. Shopping for the girls' back-to-school clothes. At the Woodland Park Zoo as they'd stood back and watched the girls try to get a hippo's attention. He'd reached for her hand and she'd felt the purest kind of contentment. *Family,* she'd thought. The notion scared her, because she wanted it so much.

"I've fallen in love with you, too."

It had happened fast. Eight weeks ago, they'd been friends. Not even particularly close friends. Just adults thrown together by the bond between their daughters, who had been besties since third grade. After Hunter's wife was killed in an on-base attack in Afghanistan, three years ago, Hunter's deployment schedule had left Clara primarily in her grandmother's care. In Trina's world, Hunter had been a mostly absentee dad who occasionally dropped off and picked up his daughter with a smile and a hug.

And then—

"I've never felt this way before."

Hunter's words. The words she'd wanted to say, the words she'd been thinking, coming from his mouth, getting under her skin, soaking into the pulse of her blood.

"Not even—" He'd been married to Clara's mother for eight years before her death.

"No. This is different."

"Me neither." She couldn't muster more than a whisper.

He sat up, pulled her upright, and took both her hands. "After I come back—"

More words she hadn't let herself hope she'd hear. She'd been willing to wait, to let the way she felt, the way she knew he felt, stand on its own. To have faith in the strength of what had passed between them, without outright declarations. But here he was, promises in his dark brown eyes.

"You're going to be living in my house anyway—"

Trina had offered to watch Clara for him during his year-long deployment. Hunter's mother had met the man of her dreams, a Honda Gold Wing–style wanderer, and gone off to see the country for the first time in her life. For Trina to care for Clara alongside Phoebe wasn't much trouble—the girls were easier together than solo—and a grateful Hunter had asked her if she'd like to house-sit. He politely hadn't said anything to indicate he'd noticed the shabbiness or cramped quarters of her and Phoebe's digs. She'd jumped at the house-sitting offer. Only an idiot would have turned down the opportunity to live in Hunter's big house in the Grant Hills woods instead of in her one-bedroom rental, especially with two girls on the brink of adolescence.

Hunter squeezed her hands, his gaze holding hers. "So, I wanted to know: Can we make it official? Will you move in with me? Like, for real?"

"Yes!"

He laughed. She hadn't hesitated or played coy, and maybe if she'd taken a second to reflect she could have at least pretended to think about it, but the truth was, she was no good at pretense, and had never seen the point of it with Hunter. He made her want to be *Trina,* exactly who she was when she woke up in the morning, without ornamentation or decoration. And that was—she knew without doubt—who he'd fallen in love with.

It was the most amazing feeling, to be loved like this.

The way he was looking at her . . .

"I'd been thinking, anyway, even before"—he touched her cheek tenderly—"even before *you* happened to me, that this might be my last deployment. Because of Clara, partly. Even before my mom took off with Ray, I already felt like it was wrong, leaving her, without—"

His voice tightened. Trina knew he ached for his daughter and what she'd lost—as much as, if not more than, he grieved for himself. Before Dee, Clara's mom, had died, they'd staggered their deployments so Clara always had a parent with her.

"I've been doing this a long time, and it never gets any easier. Leaving Clara. Seeing what I've seen . . ."

Sitting by the outdoor fire pit one night after the girls had gone to bed, side by side in their sleeping bags on Clara's floor, he'd told her this last deployment had been the hardest yet. He'd said that he'd thought it would get easier eventually, but it never did. Men were lost. Mistakes were made. They were the most human, humble mistakes, but the consequences were enormous. Civilians killed. Families and cities broken. Hearts, too. That was the thing, he said. If you stayed in long enough, you would almost certainly come home broken, if not in body, then in spirit.

"I've served out my obligation. I'd like to come out and . . . and be here with Clara. And you and Phoebe. We could be together."

She didn't think she could stand it, how full she felt, and maybe he saw that in her eyes, because he reached for her then, leaned forward and took her face in both his hands and kissed her tenderly, gentle for that first contact but then hot again, right away. His fingers moved through her hair, over her neck and shoulders, his breath hard and fast already, mingling with hers. The kiss was almost brutal, his tongue invading, one thumb and finger urging her nipple to standing, and his voice low in her ear said, "I didn't think I could want you again this bad that fast."

After a second round of lovemaking, they lay for a long time, silent, and then he told her what he'd been thinking, that he'd leave the army and maybe pick up the finish-carpentry work that he'd done summers in high school and between deployments. He built a fire, and she watched from the blanket, loving the Boy Scout/soldier/*man*liness of it, and they made a plan together. She'd sleep in the guest room when he was away and for a little while after he came home, because the girls still didn't know anything about what was going on between their parents. There was nothing new love needed less than the scrutiny of two eleven-year-old girls. But then after he'd been home a bit and everything had settled down, they'd tell their daughters.

"It'll give them time to get used to all of us being together."

All of us. Being together.

She loved it. It was something she'd never had with Phoebe's father, and for the first time, she let herself believe it could happen with Hunter, her joy tinged with only the faintest fear, because they were, after all, talking about a whole year in the future. "And it'll give you time to make sure your feelings haven't changed," she said tentatively. But her imaginary fingers were crossed in hopes he'd tell her not to be ridiculous.

He rolled over and braced himself up on his elbows and looked down into her eyes, his own full of everything he'd already said to her, all the words she'd tried not to want to hear, words she'd have to save up over the next year because she'd miss him, miss this, so bad . . .

He brushed a strand of hair off her forehead, swept his thumb over her bottom lip. "I've known you a long time. Maybe we've only been involved a little while, but I know you as a person, and I know you as a mother."

He leaned in and kissed her, sweet and deep.

"I know my feelings, and they're not going to change."

Tears filled her eyes.

Those words, they were like having everything that had happened already that night, the whole vast, beautiful gift of it, tied up in a bow.

1

There he was.

Stepping through the glass gate doors at SeaTac. Striding, head up, not uniformed, as she'd expected, but clad in jeans, a gray T-shirt, and hiking boots. A backpack slung over both shoulders.

Trina felt like she'd never seen him before, and maybe she never really had. Because *before,* he'd been somebody's dad. Somebody's husband. And then friendship had morphed into love, so she'd never had that first-time-I-laid-eyes-on-you, love-at-first-sight moment. No heart stopping, no breath catching, no hormones firing in one big surge—

Not till now.

Because, *damn.* Dark hair and dark eyes, stubble smattered over his jaw, shoulders that poured off strength. Six-foot-plus of him, moving with intention. He was a guy who'd catch your eye on the street, pheromones setting you back on your heels before you'd registered that you'd turned to look. The hardness of his features, the everyman handsomeness,

made an impression only after it was too late to decide how
you felt about his appearance.

There were more lines in his face than she remembered
—the laugh crinkles at the corners of his eyes, yes, but deep
lines in his forehead, too. His eyes combed the crowd, looking
for someone.

I'm right here.

Then his gaze swept past her and locked somewhere else,
and his pace quickened until he was almost running. Behind
her, someone broke away, flip-flops smacking heels.

"Daddy!"

Clara ran to her father and threw herself into his arms,
forgetting Trina's and her grandmother's warnings to be gentle
with him. Clara was laughing and crying and trying to tell her
father everything that had happened in the last year, all at once.

"Slow down, baby." Hunter knelt so he could hug Clara in
earnest. "Slow down. We'll have plenty of time." He was smiling, looking so much like the man Trina remembered, and
she realized she was silently pleading for him to raise his eyes
and search her out. To turn that smile on her. And she shook
her head, because this moment wasn't for her. It was for Clara
and Hunter. Trina would have her moment later. When she
and Hunter were alone.

Hunter raised his head, and her heart skipped.

But his eyes caught on something behind her, and he rose
and strode forward: "Mom."

Trina wasn't going to panic. She clutched her WELCOME
HOME, HUNTER sign tighter, and tried to slow her pulse down.

Homecomings are weird, Hunter's mom had told her when
Trina met her flight several hours earlier. *Don't get your expec-*

tations up too high. He'll need some time and space, and then it'll be like he never left.

Plus, Trina had known they'd have to play it a little cool, to maintain the fiction for the girls.

In the meantime, Trina would remember what he'd said to her. Not only *I love you,* but also, *I know my feelings, and they're not going to change.*

Hunter's mom, Linda, was getting the full Hunter. Or the half Hunter, maybe, because Trina was pretty sure that Hunter at full strength would have swept both mother and daughter off their feet. Certainly in all her fantasies he'd swept *her* off her feet.

But with his chest wound just barely healed—a wound that had almost killed him—he wouldn't be sweeping anyone off her feet for a while.

A hand snaked around her waist. Phoebe, at her side. Her daughter, awkwardly twelve and yet so beautiful, with that coltish mix of woman and little girl.

Phoebe was clearly feeling as awkward and left out of this homecoming as Trina was, and wanting solidarity.

That was the moment when Trina started to feel really, truly freaked out. Because she was fine with the fact that homecomings were weird and fine with Hunter's priorities being for his daughter and his mother and fine with the secrecy that they'd agreed to keep up a while once he got back, but—

He hadn't made eye contact with her. Not once.

Something was wrong. Even Phoebe could sense it.

And all at once, the worry that she'd been holding at bay coalesced into a solid block in her chest. She had to fight it back so she could smile down at her daughter, an arm around her, and squeeze her reassuringly to her side.

I know my feelings, and they're not going to change.

For the first few months after Hunter had left, it had been so easy to believe, unswervingly, in their happily ever after. She'd had letters and emails, reminders of his devotion. Sometimes even instant message sessions in which they'd planned and plotted—where they'd have dinner, the movies they'd see, the places they'd take the girls, what, in detail, he'd do to her in bed—*when he got home.* She'd felt their intimacy deepening through all of that, as he confided his doubts and his fears—a squad mate in danger of losing his shit, an unspecified plan from on high he couldn't completely get behind, one too many small failures of his immediate leadership.

And, over and over: *I love you. All I want is to make it through this and get home to you and Clara and Phoebs.*

Then nothing.

He'd warned her he'd be off the grid for a while, on an extremely remote base where the satellite Internet connections were notoriously bad, where letters went to die. Even so, even with reassurance from the rear detachment commander that everything was copacetic, the silence had been terribly unsettling.

Then, finally, they'd had word: the notification that he'd been badly wounded in battle, which they received nearly two weeks after the fact. By the time he'd called Linda two days ago he'd been stabilized, evacuated to Germany, flown back to the U.S. to recover at Walter Reed—and booked on a commercial flight home.

When Trina had gotten off the phone with Linda, the mix

of *He's okay, he's alive,* and *He almost died* had made her ill enough to actually throw up, which she did, very quietly, out of sight and sound of the girls, in the downstairs bathroom.

She'd tried not to think about the fact that the phone call had come from his mother and not him—and after all, he was coming home—*home!*—in two days. She'd tried to call him a few times in his hospital room, but the phone had rung and rung. She'd left messages with the nurses' station but hadn't heard back. Still, she'd decided not to worry unduly. He had his reasons, she was sure—she told herself that his fatigue must be deep, the process of getting discharged from Walter Reed convoluted. There was no need to assume the worst.

But now, the fact that he'd called his mother and not her, the fact that he hadn't returned her calls, seemed ominous. It went, part and parcel, with his failure to *see* her.

"Phoebe! Trina!"

Hunter's voice, so deep that she could feel its lowest vibrations—and not only in her eardrums—rang out.

"Thanks so much for coming out to welcome me home!"

Hearty. Jovial. Impersonal, almost formal. He reached out to hug her, but in the hug, she felt the careful distance that men keep from women they're not interested in. Maybe his wounded torso was sore.

Or maybe that was a convenient theory she was clinging to so she wouldn't fall on him and beg to know what the heck was going on.

His eyes, as he drew away from her, held only a faint curiosity, as if she were someone he had once felt something for and now was wondering what all the fuss had been about.

Clara was still talking, a mile a minute, softball this and

theater that, and Hunter was beaming at his daughter proudly and asking questions. Meanwhile, Phoebe, who hadn't even rated a hug but only a hair ruffle, Hunter's huge hand almost dwarfing her blond head, looked small and lost at Trina's side. Exactly how she felt, herself.

"What's for dinner?" Phoebe whispered.

That made Trina smile for real. You could always count on kids to get down to essentials, even when there was an emotional mess around them.

"Spaghetti and pesto. Garlic bread. Salad."

"Yum. At Hunter and Clara's?"

She didn't let Phoebe hear her hesitation. "Yes." Because if they didn't go back to Hunter and Clara's, they had nowhere else to go. Trina's apartment was still being sublet. The plan had been for them to stay, and even if Trina could hatch an alternative, they'd have to go back to Hunter and Clara's to gather their things.

Trina thought, suddenly, of the voicemail on her phone from Phoebe's dad, Stefan. It was still there, a periodic reminder that she hadn't called him back.

It was an alternative. Just not an alternative she'd been able to consider with Hunter's promise so vivid in her mind.

She had to believe that promise still held. At least for now. She had to have that much faith in him, no matter how strange things felt.

Besides, she had cooked dinner, the most recent act of service she'd performed—willingly, happily!—to take care of Hunter and his daughter and his house. And maybe it was only a defense against the shards forming in her chest, but she got mad. Because no matter what the hell had happened to him over the last eight months, he'd said those things to her. And no matter how tough the last year had been for him, he owed her more than a formal thank you and an awkward hug. It wasn't the changes she'd made to her life that bugged her so much. Quitting her jobs, moving into his house, and accepting the generous stipend he'd offered for Clara's care—those were just economic decisions, and although it would take a while for her to get her feet back under her, she'd do it. No—the harder part was that she'd allowed herself to love him. And trust him. Because he'd told her—because he'd *convinced* her—that it was a safe thing for her to do.

He owed her one hell of an explanation for his behavior. And if he didn't deliver it the moment they were alone, she was going to demand to know what the f—heck—was going on with him.

HUNTER STARED into the open suitcase he'd laid on his bed.

There were pieces missing from his life.

He remembered leaving Clara with his mother. But listening to his daughter's bubbling, joyful stories of the last year she'd spent living with Trina and Phoebe in his house, it had become apparent that something was very wrong.

In the space of that realization, he'd gone from confused to freaked out.

Why would he have left Clara with Trina? And why wouldn't he *remember* leaving Clara with Trina?

In the hospital, they'd asked him if he could remember the battle that had sidelined him. And he'd said no.

Retrograde amnesia, they'd said. It meant forgetting things that had happened *before* a traumatic incident. *Very common after trauma.* There had been no evident blow to the head, but the battle had been chaotic and he'd been separated from his squad. The doctors hadn't been certain whether the long period of unconsciousness that followed had been the result of bleeding and his collapsed lung or something more ominous. So they'd given him a test called a Glasgow Coma Scale and asked him all sorts of questions to determine what he did and didn't remember.

They explained that retrograde amnesia could stretch back days, weeks, or months before an incident, so to rule that out, they asked him if he could remember the events leading up to the battle, which had taken place in a small village in the north.

Yes.

He'd reconstructed everything he could. The orders he'd received, the planning and preparation, how he'd distracted his squad the night before with a Skype session with Zach Jones, the Seattle Grizzlies quarterback and a friend of a friend.

The doctors had asked Hunter to let them know if any other holes appeared in his memory, and he'd promised to do so, but nothing had shown itself.

Not till now.

Now there were holes all over the place.

His mother seemed to have spent most of the last year on the back of a Gold Wing motorcycle driven by some guy named Ray who owned a double-wide in Southern California. A guy named Ray who, ostensibly, Hunter had met and liked. If the blushes and glow were any indication, his mother was in love.

Clara had gotten involved with theater, something she

seemed to think wasn't news to him. She'd also grown an absurd number of inches and—well, she looked more sixteen than eleven. Could all that have happened in a year?

And there was that look Trina had given him. Not one look, actually—a whole series, like she was wrestling with big emotions and, more to the point, like he should do something about it.

The first time that expression had crossed her face, something had taken a dive in the pit of his stomach. The last woman who'd looked at him with that much disappointment had been Dee, his late wife. It was the kind of look you only gave someone you were involved with. Which would explain so much else—Trina's presence with Phoebe at the airport, her beautifully lettered and intricately drawn WELCOME HOME, HUNTER sign, the fact that she'd been so painfully quiet on the way home.

It would also explain the way she'd snuck looks at him throughout dinner, as if trying to figure him out, while he'd listened quietly to the girls' chatter, saying as little as possible and desperately trying to piece together the puzzle of his own mind. There must have been two battles in a small village in the north, and somehow he'd combined them in his head to make one, so that what he remembered as the "before" of his injury had actually happened at some point in a past deployment.

And if that was true, it was quite possible he didn't remember anything from the whole of his most recent deployment, or the weeks immediately preceding it.

Jesus.

How much time had he lost? How much of his life? How much of *himself*? God, that was disturbing to think about.

He'd always thought of amnesia as waking up and not knowing who you were. He knew who he was—

Or . . .

He knew who he'd *been,* more than a year ago . . .

But since then, what had happened to him?

Obviously, something significant between him and Trina. Something that had made him trust her enough to leave his daughter and house in her care. That had put that look on her face, as if he *owed* her an explanation.

What had he done? He'd been so damn careful, since Dee, not to lead anyone on. Not to create expectations he couldn't meet.

"Hunter?"

She stood behind him, her posture tentative. With those big blue eyes, heart-shaped face, and simple, straight blond hair, she looked barely out of girlhood.

There was something painful and intimate about her presence there, in the doorway of his bedroom, as if she belonged there, as if she'd stood there many times before.

"I know you need time. I don't want to push. I just— When you left—"

He felt like he was on the edge of a cliff. That if she kept talking, he would plunge over it.

"You said—"

But he didn't want to know what he'd said. He didn't want to know what he'd promised or what she expected. He didn't want to know anything at all. If she wasn't a stranger to him, she was the very next best thing, and he didn't want her confessions or her fear, the open rawness of her expression. He wanted her to close herself up and take herself away, because he was *not* who she thought he was. He didn't know that man.

He was someone else now.

"I guess I just wondered. If you thought it still could be true." She looked like she might be trying not to cry, and he cursed his lost self for whatever expectations he'd set up in her.

There was nothing for it but the truth.

"I don't remember," he admitted. "I don't remember what I said, or what we did—"

He took a deep breath.

"I don't remember any of it."

2

"What do you mean, you don't remember?"

But even as she asked the question, she understood. She'd heard stories about soldiers with traumatic brain injuries, ones who had trouble remembering what had happened before a shock, or who couldn't code new memories of what had happened since.

She felt a sudden, unwanted sense of relief. His feelings hadn't changed. He hadn't changed his mind. His mind had changed.

"I didn't think—I didn't think you hurt your head."

"I didn't think I did either. But maybe I did. I knew I didn't remember the battle. But I thought I remembered everything before. And now—everything's wrong. Ever since I got off the plane, it's like I've stumbled into an alternate reality where I'm out of sync. I think I lost a year."

He sounded like Hunter and he looked like Hunter, and there was so much fear in his voice that all she wanted to do was to put her arms around him and comfort him. But everything about his body language was a gigantic back-the-fuck-off. And as quickly as it had come, the relief vanished and she was overtaken by panic. It was one thing to imagine that something during the late part of his deployment had killed his feelings for her. It was another thing entirely to imagine that those feelings, as far as he was concerned, had never existed.

"Okay," she said. Trying to be calm. "So you're telling me that you don't have a known brain injury, right?"

"Right."

"But you think you have amnesia?"

"Well, you tell me," he said. "The last thing I remember for sure was leaving Clara with my mom on an autumn day."

She stared at him. He'd left Clara with *her,* on a midsummer day.

"I know," he said.

"But—how do you lose a year? More? Without realizing it?"

"I'm not completely sure," he admitted. "But it's all been total chaos since I was wounded, and my team is still in the middle of nowhere, and so—I guess with no one to corroborate it seemed like I had all the pieces, and it didn't become obvious till I got home that I don't."

"So you—you don't remember anything?"

"I don't remember you," he said, in a low tone of confession. "I mean, I remember you. Phoebe's mom. But—"

He didn't have to finish the sentence. A horror was beginning to descend over her. *This isn't the same man who left me.* Grief gripped her.

But that made no sense. He was here, not dead. And he was the same man she'd fallen for.

Except it didn't work like that. The man she'd known

before had fallen as hard for her as she had for him. And this man was looking at her—

Well, he was looking at her dispassionately, the way you'd look at someone who held information you wanted, but nothing more.

All those emotions, everything they'd grown to feel together, all those weeks of sliding, slowly, toward each other, so gradually that they hadn't even been able to admit it at first . . .

All those conversations, the "No, we shouldn't; it would be too awkward and we can't endanger the girls' friendship over a passing lust frenzy . . ."

All his confessions about what held him back.

All hers.

They hadn't happened to him.

It was—

It was as if she'd been alone, as if she'd dreamed those eight amazing weeks, as if she'd invented a fantasy *him* . . .

As if *they'd* never happened at all.

Standing there with the man she'd been planning to spend the rest of her life with, she felt an overwhelming, suffocating loneliness.

She gave herself a moment to wallow in it, then pushed it aside. She didn't like to feel sorry for herself. She never had. If there was a solution to be found, if research or hard work or pure stubbornness could yield results, she would *not* dwell on the downside.

"You have to go to the doctor."

"Yeah. I'd figured that much out."

"They'll know more. They'll be able to tell you if it's

permanent. I mean, people recover from amnesia, right? That's what happens in the movies. There's a big a-ha moment, right when there's some major crisis and he has to remember his past in order to avoid making the same mistake twice, or to apprehend the killer, or whatever."

He laughed, but it was a humorless laugh. "Yeah, but don't they also always have a doctor saying, 'I don't know. You could remember in a day, a week, a month, a year, or possibly never'?"

"Yes," she admitted, and they were both quiet for a moment. Then she said, "Let's not borrow trouble. Let's see what they say."

As soon as the words were out of her mouth, she wondered if they were presumptuous. *Let's. Let us. Us.*

Once before in her life, she'd let herself get used to the idea of *us.* Let herself get used to the comfort of *knowing* someone felt the same way about her as she felt about him. And once before, her life had been terribly altered by the discovery that she'd been wrong.

This was why she'd resisted falling for Hunter in the first place. This was why she'd kept their relationship a secret from the girls all this time. Because you couldn't count on *us.*

Hunter had convinced her you could. He'd made her believe it. But he'd been wrong.

"So we were . . . ?" He inclined his head questioningly.

"Involved. Yes."

"How involved?"

There was something charmingly male and guileless about the question that made her half smile, despite how lost she felt. Of course, like the thirteen-year-old boy trapped inside him, he wanted to know first off whether they'd slept together. Next, he'd want to know whether he'd been good at it.

"Very," she said, remembering their last night together and then wishing she hadn't as a wave of sadness washed over her.

For a moment there was something in his eyes. A dark glimmer. And she waited, breathless, for him to say what she hoped to hear. *We could try again.* Or, better yet, *There is something so familiar about the way I feel right now. As if I'm falling all over again.*

But then the look was gone. And all she saw in his rugged, handsome face was regret and guilt.

MAYBE IF HE weren't so tired, maybe then he'd have been able to give her what her eyes were pleading for. But ever since he'd been ripped open, he'd felt a thousand years old. It was harder to catch his breath. His blood seemed to surge pell-mell through his veins and arteries, a feeling like an adrenaline rush but for no good reason.

"Do you believe me?" she whispered.

Maybe he should have been more cynical, more suspicious, but it hadn't actually occurred to him that she might be lying. She'd never seemed deceitful. He wasn't rolling in dough, and he didn't own anything worth committing fraud over. She wasn't asking him for anything, anyway. And there was the matter of all the other missing pieces, such as Clara's giant leap forward developmentally and his mother's mysterious relationship with the motorcycle-loving Ray. No, there was a year missing from his life, and it was at least remotely plausible that during that year he might have found his way into Trina's pants.

After all . . .

He tried to assess her without appearing to ogle. He'd always thought of her as Phoebe's "pretty mom," without any designs on her. There had always been a good reason not to look too closely or too hungrily. He was married. She was his wife's friend. She was his daughter's best friend's mother. She was a mom in a small community where word got around, a mom who appeared to have enough of a struggle to keep her head above water that she didn't need anyone tomcatting around.

And of course, he'd had very strict rules for himself about casual sex. As in, he didn't do it. Or, he didn't do it anymore. You only had to have one incident where K-I-S-S-I-N-G led to marriage and a baby in a baby carriage before you realized that skipping the *love* part of the equation could only lead to trouble.

So yeah, if he'd admired the flare of Trina's ass or the generous curves swelling her clingy T-shirt, he'd kept those thoughts dead and buried.

But when he looked at her more closely now . . .

Her big eyes and delicious mouth gave her a sex-kitten appeal that he'd somehow overlooked.

Although of course, he hadn't overlooked it. He'd apparently sampled it.

And what else?

Damn, it was frustrating. Had they been good together? What had she been like?

He knew so little about her. She'd gotten pregnant young,

but he didn't actually know how young. She'd never married Phoebe's dad, who was an actor on a well-known TV show (something Phoebe brought up as frequently as possible in conversation). Phoebe's dad had periodically sent extravagant gifts to her—he knew because Dee had told him—but didn't pay regular child support. Trina worked long hours, sometimes more than one job, to hang onto their small apartment in the highly ranked district where Phoebe and Clara went to school.

She had to be a good mom, because Phoebe was a sweet kid. Funny, thoughtful, polite, good in school, an unfailingly loyal friend to Clara.

But that was about it. That was about all he could say he knew about Trina Levine.

And yet he'd apparently had sex with her.

Very, she'd said, when he'd asked how serious they'd been.

He wondered what that meant.

Screaming passion and mutual orgasms? Or just —compatibility?

Sex that was by turns tender, fun, and wild? Or just—sex?

Imagining Trina in the throes had brought on a half-mast state of arousal and the beginnings of one of those headaches that had been his intermittent companion since he'd woken up at Landstuhl Medical Center in Germany. *Loss of blood, dehydration, shock,* they'd said.

Now he wondered what they'd missed.

"I could show you the letters you sent me," she said. "They must be somewhere. And emails. We sent each other loads of emails. You could read them . . ."

Damn, he'd never answered her question. She'd asked if he believed her.

"No," he said. It came out shorter than he meant it to. "I mean, yes. I believe you. But no—not the letters and emails. Not now. Maybe another day."

To have to read through a year of correspondence with her watching him with that hopeful, expectant look. He didn't think he could take it.

"So—what happens now?"

With a shock, he realized that mixed in with all the uncertainty, there was invitation in her eyes and voice. Of course. As far as she was concerned, they had a history.

He could have her, if he wanted. That's what she seemed to be trying to tell him.

He was human. He was male. The pleasing visuals and the note of willingness, even eagerness—they worked on him. Half-mast obediently swelled to downright—or, erm, upright—enthusiastic.

Twelve years ago, give or take, he'd followed his dick into bed with Dee. They'd been in basic together, and she'd pursued him, and he'd been flattered. They hadn't been the only pair to ignore the absolute injunction against fraternization.

If a little part of him had known that he didn't feel about Dee the way Dee felt about him, that part had been a whisper drowned by the fun and ease of regular, ready sex, the drama of doing the forbidden, and the appeal of being one of the few men he knew who was actually getting laid.

Then Dee had gotten pregnant—

And they'd had to get married. No choice, not in the army.

Slowly he'd realized. He'd sorted out what was sex and what was love. His emotions caught up to his libido. And it turned out his libido had been overeager and misguided, egged on by circumstance. But by then, he was married with a kid, committed to a lifetime. He'd accepted that—embraced his reality. He had vowed to be the best husband and father he could possibly be.

But it had niggled at him, the constant sense that there was something missing, that there was more to life, something he might never have a shot at. He'd wanted to be a better, more generous, more loving spouse and parent, but he'd often found himself wondering what the road not taken looked like.

And despite his best intentions, he and Dee had failed each other in tiny ways every day—death by a thousand cuts —until they were both worn down.

Since then, he'd been wary of moments like these, when the balance of power was all wrong, all in his hands. When a woman was willing, even eager, even though they both knew he couldn't give her what she ultimately wanted. When she was interested in more, and he wasn't.

But he'd been interested in Trina once.

Could it happen again?

He searched his soul for a sign, but all he got back were the demands of his body.

Maybe if he hadn't been so tired. Maybe if his head hadn't begun to pound. Maybe if he felt some faint tingle of *real* recognition, some sparking synapses, alerting dormant emotions.

But all he had was the sense that maybe another man in a

better state of mind, at a different place, in a different time, might have made a different decision. And all he had to offer were two words that he knew, absolutely knew, weren't the words she needed to hear.

"I'm sorry."

3

In a daze, she went back to the guest room—white eyelet lace and pale blue walls that had been Dee's taste, not Hunter's—and tried to think. It was like trying to push her thoughts through molasses.

I'm sorry.

The realization that Hunter *couldn't,* rather than *wouldn't,* give Trina what she wanted had tempered her anger, and all that was left now was grief. She'd had her heart broken once before, but she'd forgotten how sharp the pain was, and how specific. Right *there,* as if something were literally split open. And a sensation like every part of her was begging the world, *Don't really be happening this way.* Reaching for something receding into darkness.

Through the bog of her mind, a conviction leapt into clarity.

She had to tell Phoebe.

Climbing the stairs, too, felt like forcing herself through something viscous and resistant.

"Phoebs, can I talk to you for a sec?"

Both girls were facedown on their respective bunk beds, reading. When they weren't playing some kind of elaborate game they'd invented—usually something to do with improv or theater—or outside in the yard working on softball skills, this was where they were. When Hunter had first left, it had taken a while for them to see that they couldn't play together 24/7, that they would need downtime from each other, but now they sought it out as easily and as naturally as any two siblings who'd lived their whole lives under the same roof.

Phoebe, old enough now to scent danger, looked up from her book, her eyes narrowed and nose wrinkled with suspicion. "Can't you just tell me whatever it is?"

Over the last year, Trina had run this household as if the girls *were* sisters. If she had something to address, she'd address it with both of them. Sure, there had been moments that she'd taken one or the other aside for a pep talk, a heart-to-heart, or a little boundary-setting, but pretty much, she'd been able to say whatever she had to say to both girls. So it was no wonder her daughter was suspicious now about being culled from the pack for a special talking-to.

Still, there was nothing to be done about it. "Sorry, Phoebs, but I need to talk to you alone."

Phoebe slid from the top bunk and followed her mother into the hallway, her shoulders hunched.

"I need you to pack your stuff up. We're going to leave soon. Tomorrow or the next day."

"What?!" Phoebe's eyes found Trina's, big with shock, and the preteen outrage echoed off the walls of the hallway.

"I'm sorry it's so quick."

"You said—you said we'd be able to stay a while even after Hunter came back!"

Trina and her daughter shared the same fine, straight blond hair, the same heart-shaped face. But Phoebe's expression, stubbornness morphing into iron will, had come straight from her father.

She braced herself, because if Phoebe sensed room for negotiation—

"I know. But things are—complicated. Clara and her dad need to get back to their normal lives."

As soon as the words came out of her mouth, she knew they were a bad choice. The sullenness deepened on Phoebe's face. "We *are their normal lives.* You and I are Clara's normal life. More than Hunter is. We can't just leave her."

We can't just leave her.

The pain doubled and redoubled. Trina had been so stricken with grief over Hunter that she'd been blind these last few minutes to the rest of what she'd lost. Not just Hunter, but Clara, too. Who'd become a sister to Phoebe.

A daughter, to her.

She put a hand to her chest, as if she could soothe or contain the pain, but it was too great.

She got angry again, not at him, but at herself, for how foolish she'd been. To think Hunter and Clara had been hers to keep. When she should have learned . . .

Phoebe made a small sound, tugging Trina's attention back. Her lower lip was trembling, and Trina, who remembered how that lip had always done exactly that before baby Phoebe burst into tears, knew that her daughter's anger was just a shell. Phoebe was as heartbroken as Trina at the thought of leaving.

And sure enough, one tear ran down Phoebe's face, and Trina thought for the ten thousandth time in the last year that a girl of twelve was stuck precisely halfway between woman and child. "I don't want to go." Phoebe's voice was as trembly as her chin. "I don't want to go back there."

She was talking about the apartment.

"It's so small. And dingy. It always feels dirty."

Trina understood what Phoebe meant. They'd always kept it clean and neat and scrubbed, but you couldn't make thirty-year-old Formica look as glossy and beautiful as the faux granite stuff in Hunter's kitchen. You couldn't do much about floors that desperately needed to be resanded and refinished. And if the landlord stubbornly refused to let you repaint and kept delaying the work himself, the walls would eventually show fingerprints and the grime of years. It had always felt dirty, and when Trina had moved into Hunter's house she'd felt the weight of that burden—which she hadn't quite known she carried—lift off her shoulders. She'd even warned herself not to get too used to it, in case—well, women born since the last quarter of the twentieth century knew not to stake too much happiness on things they couldn't afford to pay for themselves.

But what she hadn't counted on was how it would feel to have Phoebe tell her that what she'd given her all those years hadn't been enough.

"There's nothing wrong with the apartment."

Her voice had come out testier than she'd intended, and she saw Phoebe's eyes narrow. "Really? Are you saying you'd rather live in that dump than a place like this?"

That dump.

Her chest felt like there was lead in it, but she shoved the sensation away and went on.

"Phoebe, hon. I'm not sure we're even going back to the

apartment. I don't know if we can break the sublet contract, and it's not up for another six weeks. I'm thinking we might go stay with Bonnie for a little bit."

Bonnie was Trina's closest friend, someone she'd waited tables with for years at Mike's Down Home.

"Bonnie's apartment smells like cigarettes and wet dog." Phoebe was crying now. "I don't want to go there. And Clara needs us. We can't just leave her. You're like her *mom*."

"Phoebe. Baby." Trina hugged her tight, resting her face against the fine silk of her daughter's hair. Under the darker scents of adolescence, she could still find the baby scent of her Phoebe, and the tenderness that sprang up in her was the deepest emotion she knew.

She had to listen to that tenderness now, not the part of her that wanted to cling to this house and family that weren't —and now would never be—theirs. She had to keep doing what she had always done for Phoebe—building a life for the two of them.

"I'm not her mom."

The words hurt to say, but she pressed on. For Phoebe's sake, she wanted to be matter-of-fact, to make this seem like the most normal, the safest, thing in the world. "I'm your mom. And I need to do what's right for you and me. And right now, what's right for you and me— and Clara and Hunter, too—is for all of us to get on with our lives. Clara needed us this year, but now she has her dad back, and they're going to be happy. And so are we. I promise."

But even as she said it, even as Phoebe snuggled closer, still young enough to believe in a mother's omnipotence, she thought of Hunter's promise, spoken with so much conviction, felt fully in the depths of his heart, but not his to make, or keep.

"HERE'S THE THING." Dr. Stephens, the neurorehab specialist Hunter had been referred to, crossed his arms over his barrel chest. "Just because you're passing cognitive tests with flying colors and we can't see anything on the scans doesn't mean you didn't have a mild traumatic brain injury."

Several hours of tests had brought on one of Hunter's headaches, and he really didn't need short, bald Dr. Stephens to tell him the news he'd just delivered. He pretty much already knew that somehow, somewhere along the way, he'd suffered a head injury.

"I don't have access to all your records from the field clinic or Landstuhl, which might help me get to the bottom of this, but it's *not* uncommon to miss a mild-to-moderate TBI in a situation like yours where there was battle and another serious injury and transport from one treatment facility to another. There's a military concussion evaluation, but it relies on subjective recall, which means if there weren't people around to corroborate your memories of the events, we don't know exactly what happened. And it's affected by fatigue, which ninety percent of soldiers are suffering from ninety percent of the time, and has a low sensitivity when it's administered more than twelve hours after the incident. Because of the situation you described—collapsed lung, airlift, surgery, longer-than-expected unconsciousness—it almost certainly was. And the Glasgow Coma Scale—same kind of thing. It's a subjective assessment. If data about the length and cause of unconsciousness is faulty, you're going to get equally faulty conclusions."

"But how did I make it all the way back home without someone picking up on the fact?"

That was the part that really got to Hunter. Not just that he'd lost a year, but that he'd lost it so completely that he almost hadn't known it was lost. Was it possible that if it hadn't been for Trina, he might not have figured it out for even longer?

"It's more common than you'd think," Dr. Stephens said. "Again, it's a subjectivity problem. We don't have foolproof ways to determine what someone does and doesn't remember. There are certain kinds of questions that help—asking people about recent current events, that kind of thing—but it turns out that a very large percentage of people are oblivious to recent current events, particularly if they've been in a remote location."

Hunter sighed.

"As I gather you were."

He nodded.

He'd gone to the base first thing this morning. Before referring him to Dr. Stephens, the base doctor had told Hunter he could make a case for medical discharge. "Any cognitive impairment. Which memory loss is."

But Hunter didn't know whether he wanted medical discharge. How did you decide what you wanted to do with the rest of your life when you didn't *know* what your life was like?

It was strange that all through his time in Germany and D.C., he'd never felt as disoriented as he did now, as if finding out about the gap in his memory had brought it into being.

He'd pocketed the paperwork and the referral and gone to see the rear detachment commander, Captain Carmichael. Carmichael, brand new to his position and harried, had pulled the incident report, but it had been—typically—short on details. There had been a firefight. No other U.S. casualties. No mention of insurgent casualties, but that didn't mean there hadn't been any.

"Can you find out more?"

"I can try," the captain said. "But you know how it is. Communication is intermittent. Even if they're getting email right now, no guarantee someone's got time to fill in the blanks for you."

"Tell them I lost a fucking year," Hunter said.

The captain gave him a look caught halfway between sympathetic and *tell me a story I haven't heard before.* "I'll do my best."

That left him, for as long as it took to get answers back from the front, with this giant *hole* in his psyche. And only Dr. Stephens to help him guess at what lived inside it.

"So—what?" he demanded of the neurorehab specialist. "So we have no idea what happened to me and—"

"Well, we know certain things. We know that if there was a percussion injury, like a blast, it wasn't intense enough to cause eardrum rupture. So that helps us a little. And if there was a blow to the head, it didn't cause external bleeding or someone would have flagged it. So we're probably looking at some kind of blunt trauma, which means damage—if it exists at all—is probably localized to point of trauma and point of rebound—" At Hunter's blank look, he clarified. "The point where the brain bounced off your skull on the other side."

"Oh," said Hunter unhappily. "And what do you mean,

'damage if it exists at all'? I can't remember a year of my life. That means there's damage, right?"

"Probably," said Dr. Stephens. "But it's also possible to have some retrograde amnesia in response to severe bodily injury or psychological trauma. I'm sure you've heard of childhood abuse victims or even adult rape victims with no memory of the incident?"

Hunter nodded.

"At this point, in the absence of any concrete evidence of specific brain damage, the way we proceed is the same regardless of etiology."

Hunter gave him a dirty look.

"We do the same thing no matter what caused the amnesia."

"And that is?"

Dr. Stephens, for the first time, had the good grace to look ashamed. "Essentially, we wait."

"Let me guess. I could remember in a day, a week, a month, a year, or possibly never."

"I think that about sums it up. And even if you get some memories back, you're not guaranteed to get them all back. We do occasionally use ECT—electroconvulsive shock therapy—but that can also adversely affect short-term memory coding—"

"No, thank you," Hunter said.

"Figured you'd say that. Okay, then. I'm here if there are questions I can answer," the doctor said. "And I'd like to see you again, regardless, in a couple of weeks, just to repeat a few of the tests."

Hunter nodded.

"I'll refer you to a psychotherapist who specializes in

these issues—but he'd be the first man to tell you that he's not a miracle worker. He doesn't purport to bring back lost memories, only to deal with the emotions around the loss. He'll tell you to get lots of sleep, take it easy, eat well, exercise, and keep things as 'normal' as possible."

Driving home—at least his old Subaru wagon felt familiar, down to its rattles and shakes—it occurred to Hunter that "normal" was not at all a clear concept in this case. He couldn't exactly head back to Afghanistan and hang with his buddies, who, according to Carmichael, had another few weeks to go before they'd wind down their deployment and fly home. And having Trina in his guest room, trying valiantly *not* to look like a puppy that had been smacked with a newspaper, wasn't normal either.

Except that for Clara, having Trina around was the very *definition* of normal. He'd seen a demonstration of that last night, when he'd tucked her into bed.

"Why are you making them leave?"

When Clara had been little, coming home had followed two different patterns. Sometimes the returning parent was the conquering hero, and the parent who'd stayed behind and done all the dirty work got thrown over for the missing parent as soon as he or she walked through the door.

And then there was this pattern, which he thought of as the cat-pooping-in-your-suitcase phenomenon. He'd had a childhood pet that had punished them on returns from family vacations by performing exactly that action.

Clara was mad. Poop-in-his-suitcase mad. And honestly, he couldn't blame her. It was bad enough that he came and went without—in a child's world—logic. But this time, he'd fucked things up worse, by coming home and blowing up a world she'd come to count on.

"Everything was fine before you left! We were all friends. Weren't we?"

"I'm not making them leave," he said, as gently as he could. He almost said, "They're leaving because they want to leave." But that wouldn't be fair—not to Trina, whose hand was being forced, nor to Clara, who might shift her anger, unjustly, to Trina.

And then this morning, he'd poured shredded wheat for Clara, and she'd said, in that same tight tone, "I hate shredded wheat," and he'd felt something squeeze, hard, in his chest. He didn't know what she liked and disliked, how her needs had changed. What pet names and gestures of affection she'd decided she was too old for.

But there was a difference between not knowing and not even knowing what you didn't know. And somewhere in that gap was—terror.

Trina had come into the kitchen, wearing a butt-hugging pair of gray sweatpants and a Seattle Grizzlies T-shirt. She'd somehow instantly read the situation, and before he'd even been able to react, she'd produced a plastic container of granola and poured some in Clara's bowl, adding rice milk—which was another new thing. Then she set about putting away the dishes in the dishwasher, as if—

As if she lived there. *Jesus.*

And yet, he'd been more relieved than freaked out. So relieved he'd flashed her a smile of gratitude, and she'd given him a small, shy one back.

Having her around was weird, yeah, but it was the way Clara had lived for the last year, and kicking her and Phoebe out might be really hard on his daughter. Plus he'd missed a substantial chunk of Clara's life. Trina knew things about his daughter that he didn't—not just what she ate for breakfast, but what she'd want to pack in her lunch when school started. What activities she attended. Whether she had new friends. If she had started to get crushes on boys . . .

Last night, after he'd confessed that he didn't remember their time together, Trina had told him she was going to try to be out of the house by dinnertime tonight. At the time, that had seemed like a blessing. But now he wasn't so sure. Maybe he could ask her to stick around for a few more days. To get Clara settled, help him come up to speed. Ease the transition.

Yes. He'd ask her for a few more days. Just until he and Clara could build the *new* normal.

After Hunter left for the base, Trina dug into the problem of where she and Phoebe would go next.

By late morning, she was starting to panic. Bonnie's sister and her five kids were coming to live with Bonnie for an indefinite period of time because her sister's deadbeat husband had allowed their house to go into foreclosure. There was no room in Bonnie's little house for Trina and Phoebe now, even if Phoebe hadn't been spot-on about the choking smell of cigarettes and wet dog. Trina's parents were dead, gone one after the other, right after Phoebe's eighth birthday, and Trina's siblings lived on the East coast, so begging family for temporary lodging wasn't an option.

Trina had somehow lost the phone number for Petra, the woman subletting her and Phoebe's apartment, so she'd emailed the friend who'd put them in touch in the first place. She'd given a sketch of the situation, without getting into the romantic thread: Deployment ended sooner than expected, house-sitting opportunity brought to a sudden close, in need of a place to live again.

I can't tell you what to do, her friend wrote back, *but before you call Petra, you should know that her son has leukemia. I think he's doing well, I think he's going into remission, but she's been dead on her feet for months now. I know you, and I know what a soft heart you are, and that by telling you this I might be forcing your hand, but I also know you'd kill me later if I didn't tell you.*

Trina didn't call Petra. Her friend had been absolutely right about all of it. Trina was glad to know the situation, and there was no way she was going to retake her apartment, given the other woman's suffering. She and Phoebe would figure something else out.

Swallowing her fear, she began searching sublet listings online. Most of the apartments were small. Ugly. In a bad part of town. Or way out of their price range.

She picked up the phone to call about one that seemed promising. Gone. The apologetic landlord said he'd heard nothing stayed available more than twenty-four hours right now. That if the date on the listing wasn't today, there wasn't much hope.

The possibilities were few and far between. It had taken months for her and Phoebe to find the apartment they'd been living in—part of why she'd sublet instead of bailing on the lease entirely.

Maybe . . .

Maybe she could ask Hunter to let them live in the guest room and pay rent?

The thought of being in the same house as him while he looked at her with that blank indifference hurt her stomach.

She'd spin back through the apartment listings she'd already looked at and be less picky. They could handle small. They could handle ugly. They'd have each other, they'd keep busy, they'd spend time with friends.

Where had that one gone . . .?

She clicked on the browser's history. Scrolled . . .

Through apartment listings and page after page of Stefan Spencer.

Phoebe had been doing online searches for her father. Looking at every photo in existence. Reading every article ever written. Watching trailers from his show.

She shouldn't be surprised. Not after that voicemail from Stefan.

She swiped her phone to life and tapped the voicemail icon.

"Phoebe's emailed me a couple of times. She's a funny kid. I— I'd like to get to know her a little better. I don't suppose there's any chance L.A. is still in the cards for you? There's an entry-level job available on the show that would involve at least part-time work on set design. I think it could be a chance for you, if it's something you still think about. I've got a friend whose apartment will be available the next month or so; you and Phoebe could live there while you looked for a place to stay. It would mean a lot to me. I know I've been a shit father, but I've grown up a lot and I'm ready to do better."

She'd almost deleted the voicemail unheard. Then she'd listened and almost deleted it again. But she hadn't. It was still on her phone. And suddenly it seemed like a very different proposition.

She'd met Stefan in high school. They'd done theater together, and bonded over their shared plans to head to Hollywood after graduation.

Stefan was gangly, an unlikely leading man—until he wasn't. Until he came back to school the fall of his senior year after a summer of working on his grandparents' Iowa farm. The sun had cured his acne and tanned his skin, and manual labor had put muscle on his frame. Trina had had trouble looking away. Plus, he was still her friend Stefan, the one she'd conspired with about sharing an apartment after they both managed their escape to Tinseltown.

Then he got the part of Harold Hill in *The Music Man*.

Up there, on the stage, strutting and commanding—

Night after night, wooing and winning over the audience, softening them up until they were putty in his hands—

And finding his confidence, his own best self, of course.

Trina was a *goner*.

She made up her mind she'd have him.

Only thing was, she had Marian for competition. And Marian was up there onstage, being kissed, having Harold's— Stefan's—arms around her. So Trina needed a trump card. And she had one. Marian was a good girl. And Trina wasn't.

After cast parties, when Marian the Librarian demurred, Trina had no such compunctions. She'd drown Stefan's adrenaline or soothe his post-performance depression, whatever it took. Kisses in the living room, blow jobs in the dark backyard of some cast member's family's house, and eventually, after some wooing, sex in the backseat of Stefan's car.

A broken condom.

He didn't see why she couldn't just terminate the pregnancy. And she got as far as making the appointment. She'd been an accidental third child, herself, her mother pregnant at forty-nine, Trina's next youngest sibling thirteen years old. In the car on the way to the clinic Trina asked her mother, *Did you think about—having an abortion?* And her mother had said, *Yes.*

And why didn't you?

I don't know. I just couldn't.

A long silence, in which Trina heard condemnation. Even at sixteen, she was old enough to wonder whether it was in her mother's voice or in her own head.

Do you think it's wrong that I'm going to?

I was forty-nine, Trina. You're not even seventeen yet. Having a baby right now will cut off so many possibilities for you.

But she hadn't actually answered Trina's question.

And in the next block of silence, Trina understood that she wouldn't go through with it.

Even though Stefan had made it abundantly clear that if she went ahead and had the baby, he didn't feel like he owed her anything.

Stefan went to L.A.

Trina had Phoebe. And fell in love.

She worked harder than she'd ever worked in her life— and that was *with* her parents' help. She waited tables and made espressos and handed clothes into the T.J. Maxx dressing room and did whatever it took to make a life for her daughter. Eventually, L.A. and Stefan drifted farther into fantasy.

Trina toyed with the rubber edge of her phone case, then made up her mind and tapped Call Back.

"Stefan. It's Trina."

"Oh! Hey. Wow. I didn't think you were going to call me back. Not that I would have blamed you."

For twelve years, they'd spoken only when money was on the line. When Phoebe's needs outstripped Trina's budget, those few but scary times. She'd told herself she'd never let her pride keep her from making sure Phoebe had what she needed, and she'd stuck to that. And Stefan, to his credit, had never, ever made her feel small for asking. He'd always said that L.A. had been good to him and he was happy to do something for Phoebe.

He occasionally invited them to visit and Trina always said no, thank you. There had been a few times, here and there. A trip to Disneyland when Phoebe was six, a tour of the studio when she was eight. But L.A. was a thousand miles away and Stefan's world a million miles from theirs. He'd never wanted things different, and after her heartbreak had healed in the joy of new motherhood, neither had she.

He wasn't a bad guy. It was just that Phoebe had changed everything for her and nothing for him, and their lives had veered apart.

"I almost didn't," she said. "But your timing was good. We're a bit—between things, here. The job—is it still open?"

"It is. And it's yours if you want it."

"I don't—I'm not sure yet."

"Do you know when you'll know? There are a few potential candidates waiting in the wings. I could probably push you to the top of the list, but I'd need to know tomorrow. You know how it goes."

She did. For a job like that, a foot in the television door, there would always be thousands of potential applicants. She was lucky it was still a possibility.

"And if I want it? When do I need to start?"

"Yesterday?" He laughed. "Definitely within a week or two. I'll check to see what the drop dead is."

"And that apartment you mentioned—still available?"

"I'll check, but I think so."

"If I give you an answer by eight a.m. tomorrow?"

"Works for me," he said.

She had only just hung up the phone when Phoebe came into the guest room, wrist extended, a handmade friendship bracelet dangling from her fingers.

"Mom? Can you help me tie this bracelet on?"

"Did Clara make this for you?"

"Uh-huh. And I made one for her."

She tied the thin strands. "Phoebe?"

"Yeah?"

"How would—what would you think about maybe going to L.A. for a while?"

"To L.A.?"

"Where your dad is."

"Why?"

"Well—there's a job there. A set design job. That's what I used to think I'd want to do."

"Before you got pregnant with me?"

"Well, when I was in high school." She tried never to make Phoebe feel guilty, like somehow she'd cut off Trina's opportunities. Because, yes, after getting pregnant, Trina had been on a different path than she'd ever planned on, but now she couldn't imagine her life without Phoebe.

Trina had barely done any designing since Stefan left—just community theater here and there when her parents could watch Phoebe.

"I miss it," Trina admitted to Phoebe. "When I worked on the tree house, I was so happy."

There was a tree house in Hunter and Clara's backyard, a fabulous one he'd built himself. Trina had taken one look inside and seen a world of possibility. She'd imagined it just like a theater set, the first time her mind had taken that kind of creative flight of fancy in *years*. And bringing her vision to life, with Phoebe and Clara's help, had been incredibly satisfying.

"It was really fun," Phoebe said.

"It was, wasn't it? Set design's like that."

And she wanted to create the best possible example for her daughter. She wanted Phoebe to see her working on something that mattered to her. A labor of love, not just making ends meet. If she took Phoebe to L.A., Phoebe would get to watch two parents do that. Surely that was worth something.

"I thought maybe you'd like to get to know your dad a little."

Phoebe shrugged and looked away.

"It's okay for you to be curious about him. It won't hurt my feelings."

Phoebe's eyes, suddenly wide and alert, found hers.

"Seriously, sweetheart. If you want to know more about him, it's okay to ask me. Or to—whatever. Search online, email him, call him on the phone—I'm not going to get mad. And I'm not going to be jealous. I know you love me."

Phoebe threw herself into her mother's arms, and Trina squeezed her daughter tight, fighting the sudden prickle of tears.

"I do. I do love you. So much."

"So, I don't know. I thought maybe—at least for a while, we could try L.A. Do you want to?"

Phoebe pulled back, looking hard into her mother's face. There was a brightness in Phoebe's eyes now that had been missing since Trina broke the news that they would be leaving Hunter's house immediately. A curiosity, an interest.

Trina's heart unfolded with gratitude as Phoebe nodded.

4

He found Trina in the guest room, packing her suitcase.

She looked up from the nightgown she was folding. He couldn't help the way his mind leapt from the silky scrap of blue in her hands to an image of the negligee draped over her generous curves.

Whoa.

A fantasy? Or a *memory*? Had he seen her in it before?

He couldn't remember ever glimpsing her in anything other than jeans or cutoffs and a T-shirt. She was that kind of woman, practical, fond of serviceable things.

Or so he'd thought.

It was maddening, not being able to trust your own brain.

"You're packing," he said.

"Yeah."

"I actually came to ask if you'd stay a few days. For Clara's sake."

She turned away.

"I don't—I don't think it's a good idea."

He hesitated, but he knew how much he needed her help. He had a responsibility to his daughter.

"You're the one who knows Clara best now. Her routine. What she needs. It'll take me a little while to catch up. And I don't want to pull that rug out from under her. Because I think she's going to be pretty scared when I tell her about my memory—"

He rubbed his forehead, then told her what the doctor had told him.

She listened, then sighed. "Damn. You wouldn't think—I guess I want to think it's more of a science than it is."

"Yeah."

She was scrutinizing him, and he didn't bother to hide how freaked out he felt. He turned his palms upward. "So what do you think? Just till Saturday, maybe. Get me up to speed, give her a little time to settle into having me back with my messed-up memory? Won't you need that much time to find another place to stay, anyway?"

"We're actually going to L.A. There's an opportunity for me to get a foot in the door on set design for a TV series. It's something I've always wanted to do. Stop me if this feels like stuff you already know . . ."

He shook his head regretfully. He'd always prided himself on remembering stories his friends had told him. Remembering details, names.

She sighed. "Yeah. It just feels so weird. Telling you again." She shot him an opaque glance, then looked away. "Anyway. I was planning to go to L.A. with Phoebe's dad. Before I got pregnant, that is. And then—well, he wasn't ready. For a baby. Can't blame him. I was sixteen. He was seventeen."

Hunter's crossed arms and scowl made it clear what he thought of a guy who'd gotten a sixteen-year-old girl pregnant and not stood by her.

Her lips curved in a slight smile of acknowledgment. "That's pretty much what you said when I told you the first time."

He found that both comforting and disconcerting.

"He went without me, and I stayed here and had her. I was angry with him for a long time. But I'm over it now, and I know Phoebe wants to have a relationship with him. She's been reading everything she can find about him online. I accidentally saw her search history. I think it would be good for her to have a chance to get to know him as a person, and the timing couldn't be better, all things considered . . ."

Hunter was not at all sure it would be good for Phoebe to get to know Stefan. From what he knew of Phoebe's dad, he couldn't imagine that Phoebe had missed out on much. Besides, Hunter had seen Stefan Spencer's TV show a few times, and Spencer was a pretty boy who couldn't act. And yet women adored him—Dee had worshipped both the character on the show and the actor who played him, and so did Clara.

He bet Phoebe worshipped Spencer from afar, too, which must have been a tough parental act for Trina to follow. He'd seen situations like that—hell, he'd been in one. When Clara's mom had been deployed, Clara was always convinced that if only she'd been around, *Mom* would have let her do whatever Dad was refusing her. And he and Dee had actually done a pretty good job—despite their other difficulties—in keeping their parenting on the same page. He bet there was a lot of "If Dad were raising me . . ." in Trina and Phoebe's patter.

He wondered if Trina still had feelings for the pretty-boy prick. How much she'd cared about him to begin with. She'd said "Phoebe's dad," not "my ex," so maybe they'd never been married, but she'd definitely liked him enough to do the dirty deed at least once.

He wondered, if she went to L.A., if she'd end up sleeping with Spencer. If she'd end up falling for him all over again. The thought bothered him, and he shook it grumpily off.

"Anyway, the *short* version is, Stefan's going to help me with a set design job and a place to live . . ."

And then he'll be sure you owe him at least a really good blow job, Hunter thought. Which summoned another unfortunately vivid image.

Fantasy? Memory?

His body didn't give a crap. All the right neurons had fired, either way, and for a moment, he wished very badly that he had the power to give her what she wanted. To offer her the things that would keep her here, in his house.

But if he tried to be the man she remembered and failed, it would be worse for both of them down the line. Because while he didn't recall what had passed between them, he could visualize all too clearly what it had been like not to love Dee the way she'd needed him to. The blaming glances, the cold line of her back as she turned away from him in bed, the pointed, bitter comments. And he didn't mind all those things just selfishly. He hurt because he knew they were both missing out on something deeper. Something better.

He didn't want to ever do that to another woman. So the tease of Trina's body and that nightgown, the lure of that willingness she'd shown him yesterday, would have to stay temptation only.

Fantasy, memory, it didn't—couldn't—matter.

"I'm glad you're going to get a chance to follow your dreams," he said, meaning it.

"Thanks." She smiled wanly.

"What do you think, though? A few extra days before you go? Just to ease Clara's mind a little?"

"I just—I don't want to be in the way."

She gave him a brief unguarded look. It was that same look that had made him feel so out of sync with her before—a look of intimacy, familiarity, even longing. But this time it didn't make him uncomfortable in the same way it had the night before. This time, he *got* it. They were each alone in these parallel realities—his, in which the whole last year hadn't happened, and hers, in which it might as well not have. And it was hard to say who'd gotten the rawer end of the deal.

"Hey," he said. "You will absolutely, one hundred percent *not* be in the way. Whatever happened, however weird this is, if you want to be, you're still our friend. You're incredibly important to Clara—"

"Like a maiden auntie," she said dryly. And then, "God, Hunter, I'm sorry. You don't need me to guilt you on top of what you've got going on."

"Hey," he said again. "It's okay. This shit is real."

She tilted her head to one side. "You know, it feels weirdly good to hear you say that. You used to—you'd say that all the time."

She said it matter-of-factly, but now that he'd started to think about this whole thing from her perspective, he could imagine how it might have been. The two of them, sitting together somewhere quiet, her pouring her heart out. Him offering his brand of sympathy, which she obviously liked.

And now all that emotional support and trust, everything they'd built, suddenly gone for her.

Yeah, they'd both lost something.

"You should tell him!"

Linda had cornered Trina in the back of the laundry room, where she was folding a mountain of the girls' clean clothes.

"I can't tell him."

"You have to tell him! He has a right to know he asked you and Phoebe to move in."

Linda had gotten pregnant with Hunter when she was not too much older than Trina had been with Phoebe, and he was her only child. She could be fierce in protecting him, but this was the first time her ire had ever been focused on Trina. It was daunting. Linda was tall, five eleven or so, and couldn't hide her emotions to save her life. Put a headband and a few bracelets on her and she'd be Xena with red hair.

"It wouldn't change anything if I told him."

"It might."

"Linda, it wouldn't. I've thought about it. I even read up on amnesia on Google, and there's no evidence at all that hearing about the past helps recover memories. It's even possible that dwelling on the past may make it harder to move beyond trauma and get your memories back."

Linda looked just as fierce in her disappointment as she

had in anger. She'd been the most upset of any of them when Hunter had told the whole family at dinner what the doctor had said. It was the first the girls and Linda had heard of his memory loss, and there had been three very shocked faces around the table.

Not as shocked, though, as Linda's face had been when Hunter had told her, over the dinner dishes, that Trina was going to stay another few days and then head to L.A. They'd be there in plenty of time for the start of the school year, so she could help Phoebe with that transition.

"For a visit?" Linda asked.

"Permanently, I hope," Trina said, wondering if at some point she'd mean the "I hope" part.

The woe on Linda's face was a perfect reflection of Trina's own feelings.

"I was so happy for him," Linda said, and Trina realized Hunter's mother was about to cry. She set down the socks she was rolling and put her arms around the older woman, who hugged her back ferociously. "I liked Dee well enough, but I never thought—I never thought she and Hunter— I just think you and Hunter make such a good pair. And I love you."

Oh. Well, that was nice, and so was the lavender-scented softness of Linda's hug.

Gah, Trina was crying, too. As if she'd needed, on top of everything else, to realize that she was losing one more thing. Linda hadn't been around much this last year, but during her visits, she'd felt like family. Trina had come to think of her as, well, as a mother-in-law, and she had allowed herself to savor that. She missed her own mom so much. By the time she'd passed, Trina had felt secure on her own two feet, but the saying was true: a girl never stopped needing her mother.

"Are you sure it wouldn't help?"

"I don't want him to ask me to stay because he feels like he has to."

Trina said this very quietly against the silver-streaked red cloud of Linda's hair.

She knew Hunter, knew how highly he valued doing the right thing, the honorable thing, and she bet if she told him he'd asked her to move in—that he'd all but *promised* her his feelings for her wouldn't change—he would feel like he had to honor that commitment.

It would be even worse than his asking her to stick around *for Clara*. That one still stung a little.

Linda stepped back from their embrace and reached out to touch Trina's hair. Her eyes were sad.

"You know I'm right, don't you?" Trina asked her. "That if he knows he asked me to move in, he'll feel like he has to go through with it, and—"

"But what if—what if he remembers?"

"If he remembers, that's different, right?"

"And you'd—you'd come back?"

"If he asked me to."

But she realized that the possibility had already receded in her mind, that she hadn't made space for it in her planning. She didn't actually believe it would happen.

And, if her expression was any indication, neither did Linda. The older woman bit her lip and closed her eyes for a second.

"I'd hoped— You know, he's my only child. And Clara is my only grandchild . . ."

She didn't have to say the rest. What she'd hoped for. A new daughter and a new granddaughter. A bigger family for her only son.

It was strange to realize that she and Linda were connected in a new way, by this loss of what they'd both independently come to expect—and by being the only two people in the world who knew that it had ever been a possibility.

Trina clasped Linda's hands in her own. "You raised a good man."

Linda squeezed back, tight. "Thing is, Trina, when I did it, when I taught him right from wrong, when I taught him how to be a good man, I thought, 'I'm doing this so when he meets a woman he really loves, he can treat her right and hold onto her.' I've never seen him as happy as he was last summer. It made my heart absolutely soar. And this is—this is breaking it."

Trina let herself be drawn into Linda's soft hug one last time, let herself take what comfort she could in their shared pain, and whispered, so quietly she wasn't even sure Linda heard:

"It's breaking mine, too."

5

Trina woke in the dark, heart pounding, jolting her upright before she was fully awake.

There was a sound from upstairs. One of the girls, crying.

She turned on her bedside lamp and went to the door, pushing it open farther. She always slept with it slightly ajar so she'd hear the girls call out if they needed her. In a whole year, they never had, but she liked to know she'd hear them just in case.

She crept past the foldout couch where Linda slept—snoring like the Amazon she was—and up the steps. It seemed crazy to imagine that Clara, who hadn't wept once when her father had left for Afghanistan last summer, might be going to pieces now over the thought of a surrogate mother's departure. But Clara had been even more upset than Phoebe when she'd learned that Trina was leaving, and not at all ready to embrace a few extra days as a consolation prize.

And someone had called out in the night.

It came again, another cry, and she hurried upstairs and into the hallway. She pushed the girls' door open and peeked in. The nightlight in the hallway cast enough of a glow into the room that she could see that both slept soundly, not moving.

Maybe she'd imagined it. Or dreamt it. She'd woken from a deep sleep before, certain she'd heard a sound, only to be unable to trace its source.

She closed their door quietly behind her and started back toward the stairs.

She heard it again.

A groan. A sound like a broken half *no*.

Hunter.

He was alone in there. Asleep, dreaming.

She knew soldiers back from deployment often had terrible nightmares, even the ones who hadn't suffered physical trauma.

She also knew she should continue toward the stairs. She had no right. No right to intrude into his bedroom, into his sleep, into his dreams.

But his voice came again, strained, like something not quite human, utterly ground down, and the sound of him suffering mattered to her more than the fact that he couldn't remember her or that he'd pushed her away. It was more primitive and more important than her pride.

She turned his doorknob slowly and went in.

He'd gone to sleep naked, or mostly naked—she thought he might be wearing underwear, but she couldn't tell because he'd twisted the covers around himself, and he was fighting against them. In the nightlight's dim glow, a sheen of sweat covered his skin, and his face was contorted with terror.

I should leave.

But she didn't, and when he cried out again, she didn't think, she just climbed onto the bed with him and put her arms around him.

"Shh. Shh, Hunter. It's okay."

He made a muffled, startled sound, and in the almost dark he turned to her and lifted his face to hers. Took her mouth without a word.

In that mysterious middle-of-the-night time, outside of rational thought, she didn't protest or try to stop him or ask him what he thought he was doing. She just pressed herself closer to him and wrapped around him tighter and opened to him. And it was so familiar, the pressure, the heat, the taste of his mouth. The sounds he made—relief, hunger, demand. More grunt than groan, but only barely, and his arms were around her, too, his hands in her hair, on her face. The kiss so dark and sweet, so full of emotion, that tears welled up in her eyes, until she could taste salt.

Then he broke it off.

"Shit. Trina. I was—" He sat up abruptly. Reached for the lamp switch.

She scrambled out of his bed and stood, blinking in the light.

"You were in my bed."

"I'm sorry. I'm so sorry."

His eyes were startled, the pupils huge, though from desire, shock, or the sudden light, she had no way of knowing.

He was shaking his head. "What—?"

"You were asleep. Having a nightmare. And I—I wanted to help, and I didn't think. God, you must think I'm—"

"No. No."

Her face was hot with frustrated desire and fresh humiliation. She covered it with her cool hands.

He reached for her hands and pulled them back, one by one, from her face. Took them in his and shook them as if to restore her to her senses. "I know I have nightmares. They told me in the hospital. The nurses would come sit with me sometimes."

"I—"

"Trina—"

"No, I'll go."

"Wait."

If he hadn't been holding her hands, she would have been back in her room by now. Anything to get away from him, from the pity in his eyes. Anything to get away from what she'd done—taken advantage of a man who was asleep, suffering, a man who'd made his feelings about her plain enough.

"Trina, this is a fucked-up situation. There's no road map. We're going to make mistakes."

"I—I can't believe I did that."

"Trina, stop beating yourself up. I did it too."

"You were *asleep*."

His gaze tugged away from hers, sought refuge in a corner. "Not the whole time."

The words hung there in the halo of the bedside lamp.

"Why—why are you telling me that?"

For a long moment, his eyes held hers, and something blazed hopeful and bright in her chest. Then his gaze dropped.

"I don't want you to blame yourself. I don't want you to feel like you accosted me and I'm some victim. We both—reacted. We both made mistakes. We're both feeling our way. We can agree to forget it happened, okay?"

What a strange choice of words. *Forget.*

What she'd done had been wrong. She shouldn't have come into his bedroom. She shouldn't have climbed into his bed. She shouldn't have touched him when he was powerless to give her permission.

But she wouldn't *forget* that he'd responded.

She wouldn't *forget* the way he'd kissed her, or the sounds he'd made, or the way his hands had felt on her hair and her face.

"We can pretend it didn't happen."

If he saw the vast difference between forgetting and pretending, he didn't say anything.

And it wasn't until she was lying in her own bed again, touching her lips, puffy and tender from his kisses, the stroke of his tongue still tingling along hers, that she said aloud what she'd been thinking:

I can't forget, Hunter. I can't ever forget.

WHEN SHE WAS GONE, he eased himself slowly back down on the bed.

What had just happened?

She'd heard him cry out. She'd come in, gotten into his bed, and put her arms around him. And then—

He'd half-woken from sleep and in that almost-dream

zone had known her completely. Had found her utterly familiar and sought her without hesitation, his mouth desperate for hers.

He'd known how they kissed, that she liked this much pressure, this much tongue. He'd known what her hair felt like between his fingers and what her tears tasted like when they slid along his lips.

And then he'd struggled fully to wakefulness and her face was a near stranger's face, the silk of her hair unfamiliar. Something in him recoiled and he was beset, suddenly, by that awkwardness that had occasionally overtaken him mid-encounter in his sexually busier days, particularly with women he didn't know well. When he'd let things go too far and then come with a snap to his senses—fading drunkenness or a ringing phone breaking the spell.

It had been like waking from a dream of love to the reality of solitude.

He let himself drift back toward sleep, and in those vague, cloudy moments just before he lost himself, there it was again, like a half-remembered dream.

He could taste her, feel her against him. A vivid, desperate craving rose in him.

What kind of voodoo was that?

He couldn't remember her consciously, but some part of him knew her. The dream part. His body.

And, God. Had it always been like that between them? Because if it had, he understood why he'd let it happen. That wasn't the kind of attraction any man resisted, not for long. It was only that jarring sense of waking from a dream—and his confusion—that had put the brakes on.

If he hadn't sat up and turned on the light—

He'd been seconds away from sliding his hand down and finding her bare thigh. Pushing up that scrap of insubstantial silver nightgown to discover what she wore underneath. From what the faint light had hinted at, he seriously doubted he'd find anything.

He would have brushed the slippery fabric away from her smooth skin, slid his palm up the inside of her thigh until he found the crease where her leg met her body. Until his thumb found the softness of curls—

Memory, or fantasy, that she kept a landing strip of neatly groomed hair?

Memory, or fantasy, that she got wet enough that slickness sometimes covered not just her outer lips, but her thighs, too?

Memory, or fantasy, that when he parted her and slid his thumb along her seam, her clit would be already swollen and throbbing?

His hand was on his cock.

In his vivid inner world, she made a soft sound of pleasure and assent when he kissed her and touched her at the same time. She licked his mouth as he circled her clit. She sucked his lip when he slid two fingers inside her without stopping that insistent circular motion.

His cock was at full attention, rock hard and demanding, a drop forming at the tip that he spread over the head and down, wishing it were her hand, wishing it were her mouth, her tongue, her wetness. His fist tighter now, the grip harsher, speeding up, his breath fast and ragged, too.

Maybe memory, the sound of her breathing in his ear. Maybe fantasy, the way she begged him to fill her, yanked him against her, deeper, harder, faster. Maybe memory, the way she felt clenching around him, or maybe fantasy—it hardly mattered, because either way, she took him with her over the edge, and in the strange place between waking and sleeping, between dream and reality, he came, hard, shaking and trembling with the force of it.

6

Things had moved. He couldn't find the gas can for the mower. He felt a surge of irritation with Trina for moving his shit. And for taking the girls and going to the mall and leaving him to his own devices. And then an even sharper surge of anger at himself, because he was not that guy. Not the one who'd get pissed at someone who'd given up a year of her life to help him out, and not the one who needed her help to mow the fucking lawn.

The can was on a shelf at the back of the garage. He didn't recognize the shelf, but he recognized his own craftsmanship, meaning he'd built the shelf sometime in the fog lost to amnesia. *Jesus.* It gave him the creeps, the way things could fall into that gulf.

The mower itself was a different model than he remembered. With the old one, he'd yanked the cord and it had started. This one wouldn't start.

A slow ache crawled across his skull. He rested his head on the handle of the mower.

His left hand clutched two rods together and his right

reached for the cord again. The mower started up with a roar that he felt like relief.

Dr. Stephens had told him there was more than one kind of memory. This kind was called . . . *procedural.* If you'd done something before, you could remember *how* to do it, even if you couldn't actually remember ever having known how.

Maybe that was why she was familiar under his hands in the dark, too.

He mowed straight lines into the lawn, and even with his head pounding, the simple work gave him a sense of satisfaction.

He finished the backyard, then tackled the front. His headache began to recede. Maybe it was the steady rhythm, or the mere fact of being productive.

Or the not thinking. Not trying to remember the dark, ominous heart of his nightmare, not trying to ask himself what the hell he'd been doing last night, kissing her, and then, afterward, reveling in it, when he knew how much his rejection of her must hurt.

He cut the engine.

He would have to be very, very careful not to let that happen again, not even when sleep had made him muzzy and weak. Mindless lust, as he'd proved once, was the worst possible base on which to build anything—

And *that* was assuming that he was in any position to build. When all he wanted to do was retreat into a corner, lick his wounds, and probe the lost corner of his psyche.

"You missed a blade," said a voice from the street.

He looked up to see three men on fully loaded touring bikes, stopped in front of his house. It took him a moment to recognize the speaker.

"Nate!"

Nate Riordan had fought in his squad before an RPG had laid Nate out and killed his friend J.J. Nate had been retired a couple of years, living and working at a retreat for injured soldiers and veterans on the Oregon coast with his wife, Alia.

"What the *hell* are you doing here, man?" He let himself be pulled into a hug. Nate was easygoing, loyal, competent— the sort of man every soldier wanted at his back—and Hunter had missed him since he'd left.

"We're on this crazy-ass bike tour Jake dreamt up—trust a guy with only one leg to want to go harder core than the rest of us can stomach, right? He's like, 'We're not fucking *wounded* warriors, we're weekend warriors.'"

"Two legs. Just happens one is meat and one is man-made." The guy closest to Nate—who made Nate look small in comparison—tapped his prosthetic leg, then stuck out his hand and grinned at Hunter. "Hey, man. Jake Taylor."

Hunter shook it. "Nice to meet you. I've heard a lot about you. Knew a few guys at Walter Reed who were headed your way." Jake ran the veterans' retreat. Some guys weren't ready for normal life right after getting out, and retreats like Jake's made the transition easier. Nate had spent time at R&R as a vet before he'd gotten hired there—that was where he'd met his wife, actually.

"Headed Alia's way, then," Nate said. "She's doing double duty, taking Jake's patients for him so he can kick our asses to hell and back."

"And Nate's jealous because he knows what she can do with those hands," said the third guy.

"Shut the fuck up, Griff," Nate said. "This is Griff. We let him come along to make us feel better about ourselves, and because someone has to bring up the rear."

Griff swatted Nate across the back of the head and the two scuffled good-naturedly before Griff stuck out his hand in greeting and Hunter shook it.

"I've got some beers in the fridge," Hunter said.

"Wouldn't go amiss." Nate grinned.

They took their beers out into the backyard and sat on the patio chairs in a half circle, facing into the woods. "How'd you know I was home?" Hunter asked Nate.

"Stopped by the base, asked about you and the team, heard the whole gory story. Amnesia?"

Hunter nodded, and sketched out the medical situation for them. Earlier this morning, he'd gone to the base to see if there was any new information from the front. Captain Carmichael had encouraged him to reach out directly to his squad mates, which he'd done, in a series of emails—but given how scarce communication had been even through official channels, he wasn't optimistic.

"That fucking sucks," Jake said.

There was a short, awkward silence while Hunter thought about that. About Jake's sympathy for him and what Jake himself had been through. Whether it would be better, if you had to choose, to lose pieces of your mind or pieces of your body. That was no fucking choice, for sure.

"Could be worse." Hunter wouldn't complain to these guys. "No big unpaid bills or paternity challenges or anything like that."

Nate eyed him doubtfully. "I call bullshit." Nate had endured weeks of traumatic brain injury symptoms, then months more of unexplained pain, until he'd gone to R&R

and met Alia, who was filling in as the physical therapist there. And she'd—well, to hear Nate tell it, she'd healed him. "That sounds pretty fucking unsettling."

Hunter shrugged. Thinking of the shredded wheat, of the gas can, of the lawn mower. Of what he knew about Trina in the daylight and what he felt at night. Fucking unsettling was a good assessment.

"What does Trina have to say about it?" Nate shot him a quizzical look.

"You met her?"

"The four of you came to R&R for a picnic and to hang with Li and me," Nate said. "Damn. We had some good conversations, too." He winked at Hunter. "I'll fill you in some time. Short version: You were obviously into her, she was into you, but you guys were in denial, and nothing had happened yet. You weren't sure it was going to, weren't sure you wanted it to. I told you life was short and you should fucking go for it. Couple days later, I got a text message from you, said something like, 'Thanks, man.' Nuff said.'"

"Did I tell you anything else?"

Nate shook his head. "You didn't have to."

Hunter looked out toward the wooded area behind the house, to the tree house he'd built for Clara a few years back.

"Hunter?"

"I don't remember," he confessed.

"Jesus," said Nate. "So . . .?"

"So, nothing."

"Nothing?" Nate raised an eyebrow.

He couldn't look at his friend. "She's going to L.A. Her baby daddy's out there."

Jake's eyes opened wide at that, and a deep wrinkle formed at the bridge of Griff's nose.

"And, what, you just let her walk away?" Nate asked.

"What else am I supposed to do? She's in love with me. I'm not in love with her. You know where that goes."

"You know, Hunt, this is *not* that different from what you were saying to me a year ago. 'I think she's in love with me. What if I can't get there?' Yeah, what the fuck happens, then? You say, 'I screwed up, I took a chance and it didn't happen, and I'm sorry, but I did the best I could.'"

Jake laughed darkly. "Do not, I repeat, do *not* take romantic advice from this asshole."

"Hey, I've done okay for myself."

In fact, Nate did have the self-satisfied look of a guy who was getting some regularly and thoroughly. So did Jake, for that matter.

Griff, however, had the twitchy look of a guy who could use a change of subject matter. "You build that?" He gestured with his chin in the direction of Clara's tree house.

Hunter nodded. "Yeah. Couple years ago."

"That's a pretty fucking nice tree house."

"Hell, yeah," Nate said. "You guys should take a look."

"What're you? Like the tree-house guy? On that reality show? What's it called?" Griff's eyebrows drew together.

Hunter shook his head. "It's just a kids' tree house."

"This is not *just* anything," Nate said. Nate wasn't going to drop it, obviously, so they headed out into the woods and Nate made Jake and Griff climb up into Clara's house. It was true; it wasn't really a kid's tree house. It had stairs instead of a ladder, for one thing, and a front door instead of a trapdoor or floor hatch. It looked a lot like a miniature house, only up in a tree. It was completely weatherproof, made of the highest-quality building materials he'd been able to lay hands on, and the one room inside had been meticulously finished—wide-plank flooring, baseboards, quarter-round, crown molding.

"This thing's fucking amazing," Jake said, putting a hand out to touch the Craftsman-style front door, with its brass knocker. "Is this a real doorbell?"

"Yeah." The attention embarrassed and pleased Hunter at the same time.

He'd built the tree house this elaborately because he hadn't want to lose touch with his finish-carpentry skills—once upon a time, finish carpentry had been all he'd wanted to do, and if it hadn't been for the fact that the home-building market had crashed and burned right when he was old enough to start his own business, he would have done that instead of joining up.

"Sam would love this."

Sam was Jake's son. Jake hadn't known Sam existed for the first seven years of his life but, according to Nate, he had made up for lost fatherhood time with a vengeance.

"Sam didn't want to come on the trip?"

"Nah. You know. Wanted to hang with his friends at home. Teenagers. What can you do? Jesus, this is nicer than the rooms at R&R." Jake stepped up into the treehouse and Hunter followed him inside.

Holy crap, it *was* nice. At some point in his missing memory, someone had decorated the *hell* out of this room. The walls had been painted sky blue, and there was a simple but beautiful white silhouette of a tree on one wall. A white daybed against the opposite wall was covered with a girlish—

but not girly, Clara wouldn't have stood for *that*—quilt and matching throw pillows. There were white wood-slat blinds on the windows, a plushy rug on the floor whose colors matched the quilt on the bed, framed posters on the walls, and a clock on a pretty white bedside table. Two sky-blue beanbags squatted side by side on the floor, not far from the double-sided desk where two girls could work face to face, with a bulletin board, organizer, and whiteboard combo on the wall beside them, and cups filled with pencils and pens within reach.

Even if he'd had the imagination to envision this as the perfect homework nook, he was pretty sure he'd never have thought of the details that made it look so cozy and service-able. He was 100 percent certain he'd had nothing to do with the mural, the quilt, or the throw pillows. And his mother, as lovely a human being as she was, had never listed interior design among her talents. No, he was pretty sure Trina had done this.

"Did you do all this? These built-ins?"

There were secret nooks and crannies hidden throughout, just because it had been a fun challenge, and shelves tucked in every corner, crammed—he was pleased to see—with books. So the girls had been spending time up here. Not that he'd resent it if they hadn't—he'd built it as much for his own reasons as for Clara—but there was something satisfying about knowing it was getting used.

"All the finish, all the built-ins. But not the decorating."

"Trina—?" Nate asked, but when he saw the look on Hunter's face, he quit mid-question. "Look at this," he said instead, and pulled back two sliding bookshelves to reveal more storage, filled with games, puzzles, stuffed animals, and knickknacks. To keep the clutter away visually.

"You could do this. Like, for a living." Griff was examining the mechanism on which the bookshelves slid, which had taken Hunter a while to work out. It had to be sturdier than the average sliding doors because of the weight of the books. "The tree-house guy does. People pay him, like, $150,000 to build a room like this. And he does hotels, B&Bs, that kind of thing."

Hunter shook his head. "It's just a hobby. A way to keep in touch with my skills."

"You planning to deploy again?"

"Not sure. Medical discharge, maybe."

"You were talking about getting out, last I saw you," Nate said. "You said eight years was enough for anyone."

There was that feeling again, like his life had branched at some point and there were two different Hunters, the one who'd done stuff in that year he didn't know about and the one he was now. How was he supposed to make sense out of it? He didn't connect with the stuff Nate was telling him about himself. It felt like a story about something that had happened to someone else.

Nate didn't press. They climbed back down from the tree and returned to drinking beers. They didn't talk about Hunter's life any more. They talked about what was going on with R&R, Jake's plans for expansion. Griff told some funny stories about bad jobs and bad dates. And then Nate said they still had 125 miles to go thanks to Jake's ridiculously overambitious itinerary.

"You got a bike?" he asked Hunter. "You could come with us."

It was tempting, for a moment. On a bike, on the road, he wouldn't have to contemplate what had been lost in the branching of his life. He could just—go. Follow someone else's plan for a few days.

But he needed to stay here and get up to speed on things. Trina had agreed to stay till Friday—enough time to help him and Clara make a transition. He couldn't leave now.

"Thanks," he said. "But I gotta stick around here for the time being. Maybe catch you guys on the next trip."

"Any time," Jake said.

And then they were gone, and Hunter turned toward the house, gathering the beer bottles up and heading inside to try to figure out what he was supposed to do next.

7

The definition of insanity, thought Trina, making her way up the stairs, was doing the same thing twice and expecting different results.

Hunter was dreaming again, that same rough, broken cry piercing her sleep, and when she slipped through the door into his room, that same agonized expression contorting his chiseled features.

"Hunter," she whispered.

She was playing it safer this time. She thought.

"Hunter."

"No!"

"Hunter!"

But he was deep under, someplace she couldn't reach him with whispers or words. She put a hand on his arm, which was warm, solid, and slick with sweat. Squeezed.

Her body answered with a squeeze of its own. His skin was hot and smooth, the muscle underneath solid and shifting as he thrashed.

"Hunter, you're dreaming again. Wake up."

And then suddenly his hands were on her, grabbing her, pulling her down. For a split second she thought of a television show she'd seen—*Gray's Anatomy,* maybe—in which the traumatized veteran had attacked his girlfriend in the night. But this wasn't that. There was no threat in him, at least not *that* kind of threat. His hands were roaming, roving, finding the back of her head, the curve of her ass, drawing her down, in, and even though a shred of her dignified self kept insisting, *You can't do this again,* she socked that smarter Trina in her self-righteous jaw and let Hunter tug her mouth down to his.

Oh, *God.*

She didn't care. She didn't care what a bad idea this was or that in half-sleep he probably didn't know who she was or what the hell he was doing. She didn't care that when he awoke fully he'd push her away, or that in the morning he'd pretend it hadn't happened. She didn't even care that it couldn't be, couldn't last.

She just wanted more of him—the succulent swell of his mouth against hers, the slick contact echoing in the quiet room, the grunt of satisfaction he'd made when she'd slid home against him, key fitting lock and turning. His rough, dream-angry hands, the sinew, bone, and equally hard muscle under her own roaming fingers, the sleepy, rich scent of his skin filling her head.

Because these strange interludes, these middle-of-the-night meetings, they were the only place she could find him. Or, really, the only place and time when he could find *her.* When she knew he recognized her.

"God," he said. Or she thought he did. And "Trina." Then again, so she couldn't mistake it, "Trina."

This couldn't make it worse. It couldn't make her feel more lost. And maybe, just maybe, it could be a bridge back for him. There was no denying the connection, no denying the hard length of him against her thigh or the gratitude in the sounds he made or the way he clutched her.

And there was no denying the relief that had washed over her as she felt his mouth on hers, heard her name spoken in that sleep-roughened voice. She hadn't realized how much she'd been holding herself together, but now he was giving her permission to let go, and she poured herself into him. Kissing him long, their mouths slick and giving, his hands now drifting down to find the hem of her shorty nightgown, sliding underneath it to cup her where she was hot and achy and so willing. He groaned, clutched her like she was the secret to something, the pressure of his palm against her pubic bone over her panties setting off a cascade of sensations that her body mindlessly sought more of, her hips lifting to him. Her voice, his name; her fingernails, his skin; her hunger, his willingness to feed and fill.

He took his hand away, gave her the whole of his body between her thighs, and she'd missed him, missed this, so much. Rocking against each other and kissing, like before the first time he'd ever been inside her when they were as horny as teenagers in alleys, backseats, behind the locked door of a bathroom in his house at night, until they'd gotten their first big break and the girls had both been invited to a sleepover party.

Everything about this was brand new and ancient at the same time, the way he ground between her legs, the tension gripping and welling up there and clutching her all over, drenching her in sweat. It was impossible to tell how much was his tongue stroking hers, his mouth setting the pace, his hands pulling too hard and not hard enough in her hair, the weight of him on her like something she'd lost and found again and couldn't get enough of, the hard, hot length through two thin layers of fabric, just the right amount of friction, the emotion pouring through her like something she'd been soaked in.

Whatever it was had gotten hold of her and tightened its grasp, sweat prickling all over her body, her hips seeking him recklessly and relentlessly, and his seeking her back. He wouldn't let her mouth go and it was like being pulled, down, down, down, the tension thrumming to a taut, helpless peak, until she was breathless and beside herself, totally out of her head. She raked his back, called his name, came with an exultant, ragged cry he suffocated with his mouth, his own groan swallowed in his chest, his body rigid over hers, his muscles locked and trembling.

He lowered himself slowly to the bed beside her, found her hand with his, wrapping hers completely, a blanket of safety, and they lay there, side by side, her thoughts a jumble, words waiting to sort themselves out. Questions. *What was that? What happens now? Does that mean—*

And in the silence, his breathing was easing, lengthening, his hand coming loose, until she looked over and saw that he was sound asleep.

8

He strolled through the woods, trying to pick out a location for a new tree house. Not every tree, even in dense forest like this, was right for it. He needed a tree that was not only tall, with relatively few low limbs, but healthy enough to bear extra weight—and to outlive the humans who were about to become its new inhabitants.

He was almost out of sight of the girls' tree house, entirely out of sight of the main house, when he found the tree he'd been looking for. A thick-trunked fir, reaching far up into the canopy, free of disease, with only a few low branches—sturdy, well separated from each other, and nearly perpendicular to the ground. As if it had been made to cradle a hideout.

He had a vision for what he wanted, but he didn't know yet what it was. It would be round and cozy—a Hobbit hole up a tree—with a spiral stairway ascending. It would blend well with its surroundings and be rough-hewn, making use of raw logs or limbs with bark still intact in places, with a wraparound deck. There'd be a woodstove at the far corner of the deck, which he could use to heat water for an outdoor shower.

It would feel so good to *build*. His job had been about destruction for way too long.

And he'd teach Clara as he went, pass along what he knew to her. That was way better, for sure, than the knowledge he'd passed along in Afghanistan. How to be wary, how to be vigilant, how to tear down, how to capture and kill.

The girls had ridden their bikes to the ice-cream shop after lunch. Trina had asked them to check in when they arrived at the shop and when they left, and they'd been forbidden to deviate from their route. "I should have confirmed with you, first, Hunter," she'd said—not looking at him.

"It's fine," he said. "You've kept them alive all year; I trust your judgment."

I don't, however, trust mine. What the fuck happened last night, Trina?

If it had been a dream, it had been realistic enough to leave him with physical evidence; he'd tossed his boxers into the laundry, unease weighing heavily. He'd showered, finding other signs, a sore spot on his thigh, a chafed area where he didn't think his fist had done any recent work.

Her mouth slick under his, her body arching, her voice a choked cry.

He wrenched his attention back to the tree, his creation slowly revealing itself, his mind already leaping ahead to measurements, to the attachment bolts he'd sink, the brackets he'd need—a trip to the lumberyard in order soon.

"Hunter?"

She was tromping toward him through the woods, laughing.

"What are you doing? You look like—you know that scene in *Winnie-the-Pooh* where Piglet and Pooh are chasing their own footsteps around the tree?"

She wore a pair of leggings that cut off just below the knee and a long shirt that flared a little at the hips, emphasizing the gorgeous excess of her curves, and his hands were 100 percent positive they'd been all over that ass last night.

He imagined the conversation:

Um, I have a potentially awkward question for you.

Shoot.

Did we—last night—did we hump like teenagers in my bed?

Funny you should mention it, we did!

He let out a short laugh and she looked at him like he'd gone stark raving mad. Right. *Right.* He hadn't actually answered her question.

"I'm thinking of building another tree house."

"Another one? Lucky girls."

"Not for the girls. At least—I don't think it's for the girls."

"Then—?"

"I guess for me," he said. "I need—a project."

"Makes sense."

"Did you— I'm sorry, I don't remember, but—"

"You don't have to apologize for stuff you don't remember."

She'd done something different with her hair today, and it fell in loose corkscrews against the cream of her neck. An image, like a snippet of video, flashed through his mind: brushing the tips of her hair against the sensitive skin of her throat.

Memory?

His heart was pounding.

She was staring at him now, questions in her eyes, and he said, quickly, "I don't remember if I was around when you decorated the tree house—"

She shook her head. "I did it while you were gone. I hope it's okay."

"Are you kidding? It's amazing. I love it. I can see how you'd be a great set designer. It's like a movie set—for a happy childhood, maybe."

She smiled. "That's kind of what I was thinking when I did it. I hadn't designed anything in so long. You don't get many chances, living in apartments. I mean, obviously you can buy furniture and rugs, and that's satisfying to a degree, but I haven't been able to really choose paint colors, definitely not to do murals—"

"Did you do the painting?"

"The girls and I."

"The tree?"

"I did the tree."

"It's beautiful."

A blush had risen in her cheeks, and he suddenly wished he'd *seen* her last night, aside from the shadowy sense of her above him. Wished he'd seen her eyes, the color in her face and chest.

But it would be saner to wish it hadn't happened. That it had been, in fact, only a dream.

"So, a tree house for you? What for?"

"I don't know," he admitted. "I think just for the pleasure of building it. I miss it. Making something with my hands."

"Yeah," she said. "I miss it too. Having a picture in my head, making it real in the world."

"Yes," he said, with so much vehemence that they both laughed. And he felt a sudden surge of kinship with her. He'd never really found anyone else to talk to about that aspect of himself, partly because he'd spent most of his adult life around soldiers, but also partly because even in his home life, he'd been focused on survival—keeping his marriage together, making sure his daughter got what she needed when there wasn't quite enough love to go around in their household.

"Did we talk about this? Before?"

"Before amnesia? B.A.?"

He laughed. "Yeah. B.A."

"No. There was so much other stuff going on—we were focused on the girls, and on—"

The sudden pink in her cheeks made it clear what that pause stood in for.

"I knew you built tree houses, and I knew you loved finish carpentry. You said if you didn't deploy again, that's what you'd do, finish carpentry—"

"Yeah, Nate said that, too. That I was talking about getting out."

Her face, her eyes, even the tiny movements of her lashes and mouth, got very still. She nodded.

"Did I say why?"

Her gaze slid away from his.

"Because of you?"

"No. I mean, I don't know. I don't think only because of me. But maybe—yeah, maybe somewhat. Whatever. Anyway, forget I brought it up, okay?"

She turned away, her shoulders hunched. Even though the posture was meant to be self-protective, it made her look terribly vulnerable, and he wanted to reach out and touch her. Just something simple and innocent. Reassurance. The comfort of a human hand.

But he didn't.

"Hey," she said, after a moment, turning back. She'd schooled her face in the meantime and the storm appeared to have blown through. "Why I came out here. I was just looking at plane tickets. It's cheaper for us if we go Saturday."

Saturday was the day after tomorrow.

He nodded, feeling that tightness in his chest again. Before his injury, he'd heard people talk about that physical sensation, but he'd never experienced it. Now, it was a frequent visitor.

"I wanted to make sure you were okay with that."

So either last night hadn't happened or it didn't change anything. And he should be relieved about that. He *was* relieved about that.

She tilted her head to one side, and he thought she was trying hard to look like it didn't matter what he said.

"I think it'll be fine," he said.

Over the last couple of days, she'd gradually revealed everything she could think to tell him about Clara. Current favorite shampoo brand. The fact that she now liked to wear white camisoles under all her clothes. The school had told Trina to keep an eye on Clara's vision—she *might* need glasses if things got any worse. Clara had developed a crush on a boy in her math class but seemed to be over it now.

"I forgot to say, about the lunch wraps, if you grill the chicken, she rejects it. And she won't eat turkey breast.

Which, I don't know, is probably just as well, because I'm sure all that store-bought deli meat isn't good for kids anyway."

"It'll be fine," he repeated.

He did not feel fine, though. His head hurt. His thoughts were muddled. Words came slowly to him, as if he were trying to find them in a vast file cabinet, searching one folder at a time.

"I'll make chili for dinner for tomorrow night. It's Clara's favorite. And we could, I don't know, watch a movie they like or something."

"Sure," he said.

She turned and went back inside, and he watched the pretty swing of her hair and the sway of her ass. Made himself look away.

Saturday.

She wouldn't get to see the tree house go up, or not much of it anyway, since he hadn't touched the tip of a pencil to paper yet.

That tight feeling in his chest?

Regret, he thought.

And what a funny thing to regret. He had no sense of loss about those weeks she was mourning, but he couldn't quite catch his breath over the fact that she wouldn't be here to stamp her vision on the inside of his tree house.

The human mind was a marvel, he thought—what it chose to let go of and what it chose to hold onto.

9

Trina knelt on the floor of Hunter's guest-room closet, dumping shoes into the last of her suitcases. Some of these shoes had been part of her life for longer than Phoebe had, and she was way overdue to move on. When she got to L.A.—when she got to L.A. and was established in her job and making some money, that was—she'd have to get herself some better clothes. New shoes. If she could afford them. It was going to be expensive, living there. She'd started looking at apartment listings, and *whoa, baby.* She was grateful that Stefan had found them a temporary solution.

She and Phoebe were leaving tomorrow morning, crack of dawn. All that was left was the chili dinner and a viewing of *Inside Out* and one more night spent in Hunter's house. She'd promised herself—sworn, really—that she would not go into his bedroom to comfort him if he cried out. Because it hurt worse now, knowing that the same stunning heat still simmered between them but that this time, it wasn't enough to bring them together.

He'd told her—*before*—that his marriage to Dee had been bitter and confining—not because Dee was a bad person, but because they'd disappointed each other. *We never should have been together,* he'd told her. *We were only together because of Clara. Because we couldn't keep it in our pants. Sex wasn't enough.*

No. It never was. If Stefan had taught her anything, it had been that. It was a damn good thing she was getting out of here before she had a chance to forget that.

Although there was still a part of her that wanted to scream at Hunter: *I know your marriage sucked, but we* weren't like that. *Let me show you! Let me show you again.*

But if their encounter the other night in bed hadn't convinced him, she had no idea what would. He hadn't registered even a faint protest when she'd told him she was purchasing plane tickets.

It made her feel like weeping.

"Trina?"

Her name was barely a whisper. She turned to find Clara behind her, arms crossed protectively. Her heart gave a crazy squeeze.

When Hunter had first left, Trina had wondered if it would be hard for Clara. To be the *other* girl, not Trina's own. But gradually over the last year, Clara had won Trina over completely. It had been a series of tiny surrenders: The first time Clara had slipped her hand into Trina's, and a small sigh had escaped from Trina's lips, like the settling right before sleep. The first time Clara had cried in her arms, and Trina's eyes had filled. The first time Trina had jumped hotly to Clara's defense when Phoebe had taken a sisterly swipe at her friend, claws out. Mama Bear, now, to two.

Or she had been.

She supposed the process of coming to feel that Clara was *hers* would reverse itself. After all, Clara was in good hands.

"What is it, hon'?"

The voice got even smaller. "I got my period. Just now."

"Well, hey," Trina said. "That's—"

She met Clara's eyes.

"Yeah. I could get, all, 'Wow, honey, congratulations, you're really a woman now,' or—" She scrutinized Clara's face. "We could just skip that?"

Clara bobbed her head at that option.

"Do you need pads?"

"Yes," Clara whispered.

Trina dug in her packed suitcase. She'd been wondering how close Clara and Phoebe were to this moment.

"You know how to—?"

More emphatic nodding.

"Go ahead into the bathroom and try it out, and if you have any questions at all, come back and get me."

Clara disappeared with the pad squeezed tight into the palm of her hand, as if she could make it—and all that it implied—disappear. She was back a few minutes later.

"Trina?"

If Clara's voice got any quieter, it wouldn't be audible at all. "What, hon'?"

"What do I do when I need more pads?"

"Well," Trina said. "I'll give you the ones I have. And we can get some more at the grocery store or the drugstore." She remembered quite clearly how humiliating this had all been. "I'll pick some up for you."

"But you're leaving."

Clara's face looked very small and very innocent. Twelve

struck Trina as very young to be going through such a big change. It was true that Clara had started developing a year or so ago, but—it wasn't fair, girls getting their periods seemingly younger and younger.

"Your father—"

But even as the words started to come out of her mouth, she recalled the sense she'd had as a kid that only a mother—or at least *someone's* mother—could do this particular brand of work.

So many times over the last year, she'd filled in where Clara's mother couldn't. She'd attended softball games and theater performances, tucked her in at bedtime, listened to stories from the day at school. But this—

It made Trina want to cry, actually. Because she remembered her own vulnerability, how tempting it had been to just not tell her mother at all. To bum feminine products off other girls and hide the evidence of her sudden progress toward adulthood.

But Clara hadn't. She'd confided.

"I could—I could wait another few days to leave." That would give Trina time to talk to Clara a little bit about what she was going through, make sure she knew what she was doing.

"Could you? Would you?"

She'd already put Stefan off the few weeks when she'd ignored his message, and these few more days. She'd have to call him. Make sure the job would wait. Hope his patience would hold out.

But she didn't think she could walk away from Clara. Not now. And if she were being totally honest with herself, she wasn't quite ready to walk away from Hunter yet, either.

She nodded. "That'll give you time to tell your dad and we'll get him up to speed—"

Clara was shaking her head violently.

"Sweetie—it's not like he doesn't know periods exist."

It would be hard for Clara, entering adolescence without a mother. Trina had always known that. But she'd failed to fully realize what it would mean to Clara for *her* to leave. Her heart gave a painful squeeze.

"We'll figure this out, hon'," she said. Because that was the best she could do. She didn't know what the next step was, how you helped a twelve-year-old girl and her father navigate adolescence together. But—they'd figure it out.

She held out her arms, and Clara slid into them without hesitation, resting her fluffy red head against Trina's shoulder. And Trina felt as if her heart would break with the pleasure of that hug, the trust—enough for the two of them.

10

"I had *no* idea," Trina said. "I just thought—I guess—that you nailed a bunch of boards to the tree. I mean—" She gestured at the other tree, where the girls' house perched. "I could see that it was a little more complicated than that, but I didn't realize the planning and preparation that went into it."

For the last four days, they'd done almost nothing but work on the tree house. The part that amazed Trina was that they had only just started building the actual structure a few hours ago.

When she'd told Hunter that Clara had gotten her period, she hadn't even had to suggest that she stay longer. He'd rubbed his hands over his face, then emerged.

"This probably makes me sound like a wimp. Or like a crappy dad—"

She was already shaking her head.

"Thing is, I'm not thinking of myself. I'm not afraid of buying the stuff at the grocery store or of talking to Clara about it. But for her sake—"

"I know," said Trina, because she did. "I don't think you're a wimp. Or a crappy dad. I think you're a good dad for thinking about her."

"I know it'll be just Clara and me at some point, dealing with this. And that'll be fine. Just not—not yet. I know you're supposed to fly tomorrow morning. And I wouldn't want you to do anything to jeopardize the job, but do you think—is there any chance Stefan would give you a little more time?"

She tried to pretend to herself that her heart hadn't soared at the notion of his asking her to stay. Even if his reasons had *nothing* to do with his feelings for her.

Stefan had said that he could give her a week more. He was nice about it. But firm. A week was all. Because there were people other than him involved, and everyone was tired of getting along without help. The producers had been insistent. If she could put her butt in the chair by a week from Monday, the job was hers. If not, onward and upward.

So—on Hunter's dime—she'd paid the penalty and moved the tickets to a week later—next Saturday—and she'd laid her open suitcase on the bench in the guest room, and she'd told Phoebe they were delaying the trip. Phoebe had been disappointed for about three seconds before she'd been elated. "So we get to stay?!"

"For a week," Trina said firmly. "We're still going; we're just going to stay a little longer to help Clara and Hunter settle in."

She'd been just as firm with herself as she was with Phoebe. She was telling herself not to get her hopes up and imagine that a week's delay might stretch longer . . .

The tree house had been Nate's idea, but Hunter had snatched at it like a drowning man. Which she supposed he *was*. She knew, from observing him, how much he hated the gaps in his memory. There was a certain look he got on his face when he realized he'd stumbled into a hole—almost panic. But when it came to the tree house, it existed entirely in the present and future. He felt sure of himself, peaceful and absorbed, and Trina loved to see him like that.

First they'd spent quite a while scouting locations. She'd followed him around the backyard forest while he'd pointed out possible locations and explained the pros and cons. There were only certain trees strong enough to deal with the additional weight of a tree house, which—with the plans Hunter had bought online—would clock in at a couple of tons. Oaks, big-leaf maples, cedars, and Douglas firs could bear the weight, but hemlocks, poplars, and cottonwoods might give way, especially in wind.

He wanted, ideally, to suspend the house between two or more trees to help bear the structure's weight, and he didn't want to have to wrap it around any of the trees because it could inhibit their growth down the line. Plus, if the roof were interrupted by the tree's trunk, it would make it hard to create a waterproof seal.

After they chose a spot—well, really, after *he* chose it, while she took pleasure in watching him tromp around and pat trees and look skyward—he started setting up for construction.

He'd rented scaffolding and rigged up a complicated system for climbing the tree. A climbing harness like you'd use to scale a rock face, plus clips anchored at intervals with webbed nylon so he could "clip in" at various locations instead of always dangling. "Safer that way," he said.

"It does seem dangerous."

Although she had to confess, she enjoyed watching him climb. Her gaze clung to the stretch and bunch of muscle in his arms, thighs, and calves, the place where the harness outlined his butt and framed—

He was not hers to lust over. No matter how much it had seemed so the other night. He was not hers, and she was leaving. *Saturday.*

"I took a climbing class, believe it or not. Before I built the first one. Knot tying, self-belaying—and focused on trees and tree houses rather than rock climbing, because it's different. I mean, there's some danger, obviously, but I'm not just some Joe Schmoe weekend warrior."

And then there were the supplies. Pricey bolts aptly named "treehouse attachment bolts," or TABs, that could hold several tons of weight at a distance from the tree's trunk. Brackets that could sway or rotate or otherwise move with the tree's natural sway. Thick cables that could hold weight at even more of a distance. Oak and fir beams and planks for the platform on which the house would rest.

"You want as little contact between house and tree as possible," he explained. "Everywhere there's contact with the tree, there's friction, which means a possible wound. That's also why I need to sink the TABs so far apart. Because each TAB creates a wound, and I want the wounds to heal separately. If they're too close together, the tree might treat two adjacent wounds as one big one, and that's a big area that's subject to rot."

There was no sign, at this moment, of the uncertainty, of the headaches, of the small but real outbursts of confusion and anger. Just Hunter, competent, in control, and very, very hot.

She sighed, and tried another reset on her own desire. "How did you learn all this stuff?"

"I read a *lot,*" he said.

They were in his workshop, a shed she'd noticed a hundred times during his absence but never once entered. It was a ten-by-ten with a big workbench and several serious-looking saws and other woodworking machines. By now, there were supplies piled everywhere.

"I don't like to do stuff half-assed. I like to know exactly what I'm doing."

"Mmm," she agreed, without thinking.

He cast her a surprised look that contained, suddenly, something hot and dark. Her breath caught.

Then he looked away, and she wasn't sure it had really happened.

She'd wanted to help. So after a day or so, once Hunter had begun to talk about his plans and what he might need, she and the girls began scavenging supplies. They pored over Freecycle and other giveaway sites, and went on long trips to pick up materials. Copper roofing. Reclaimed stained-glass windows from an old church. Six-over-six windowpanes from a farmhouse scheduled for demolition. Tongue-and-groove cedar flooring. The girls *loved* scavenging. They learned to ask questions on the phone about the materials and whether it would be okay for them to "come check it out" before they agreed to take it. They learned to assess materials for soundness and appropriateness.

Clara would not, however, learn to go into Hunter's toolshed.

"I *hate* it in there. There are snakes and spiders. Big, hairy spiders."

She'd had a run-in with a spider in there that had left her terrified. She'd been watching her father work and one had crawled up her foot and—before anyone could stop it—run into the leg of her pants. It had taken hours for Hunter and Dee to calm her down and convince her that the spider was not still at large inside her clothes.

"I've refused to go in ever since."

Trina and Phoebe tried cajoling, but to no avail. So Trina and Phoebe carried the supplies into the shed, inventoried and organized, and fetched things as needed.

Trina and the girls also elaborated the interior and exterior design, inspired by what they were able to scavenge and by fantasies they spun on drives to scavenging locations and antiques stores.

"What if there were a spiral staircase up a nearby tree and then a suspension bridge?" Clara suggested.

"That sounds complicated," Trina said.

"I bet Daddy could figure out how to do it."

"I bet he could." Trina smiled, a little sadly. It was lovely that Clara's old hero worship of her father had resurfaced. But it meant that it was almost time for Trina to go. The night before, Hunter had even dared a conversation with Clara about the taboo topic, and Clara had, nervously, grudgingly, answered his questions.

As Hunter began to drill for the TABs and anchor the first beams of the house's platform, Trina, Clara, and Phoebe hatched the notion that there should be a sleeping loft. A crow's nest. An outdoor, solar-heated shower. A padded window seat with extra storage that would fold out into a bed in case additional guests came to stay.

Hunter never said no. He took the girls' suggestions seriously, and hers even more so.

"Sky's the limit," he said. "Literally."

And at night, when the girls were in bed, they sat on the couch and he told her his ideas for how he would make each item on the wish list happen, and then he sat quietly and listened while she told him what she pictured for the interior. Her focus had shifted from features to how she wanted it to feel.

"Cozy. Safe. Warm. But also not rustic. Elegant, but all those other things, too. I'm picturing autumn colors, but threads of gold. Low light, but from really beautiful fixtures. I mean, obviously you don't have to do it this way. They're just suggestions." She pushed down the wave of sadness that rose at the thought that she'd probably never see the finished product.

"Believe me, I'm happy to hear your thoughts. Interior design isn't my strong suit. And you've got an amazing talent."

"It's what I do," she said. "Set design is all about helping to tell a story, and telling a story is all about making people feel certain things at certain times. So you have an emotion in mind, and you evoke it with *things*. And being able to imagine the things and then find or make them—that's part of the skill."

"You really love it, huh?"

"Absolutely."

"You light up when you talk about it. You're—"

And then he hesitated. Touched his fingertips to his head, the way he did when it bothered him. "I should get to bed," he said.

She watched him go, and then she picked up one of the couch throw pillows and quietly cried into it.

11

She was cleaning up the girls' breakfast dishes Wednesday morning when he stepped into the kitchen.

He was wearing men's cotton pajama pants and a gray T-shirt, and her pulse leapt at her throat. Not just because the fabric of both articles was well worn and clung everywhere his body bulged with muscle or otherwise. Although it was a thing of beauty, the soft way that T-shirt knit hugged his pecs and biceps. She wanted to stroke him through the shirt so she could feel both the give of the knit and the strength underneath. And that was leaving aside entirely how very much she wanted to lay hands on those pj pants and what he was packing underneath.

No, her heart was pounding because this was the first time he'd come into the kitchen in the morning without showering and getting dressed first.

It was like *before.*

He was getting comfortable with her. He wasn't putting so much distance between them.

But it didn't matter, did it? Because she was leaving Saturday.

"Granola?" she asked, to get her head on straight, pouring him a bowl.

As she was about to add milk, he shook his head.

"You like it," she said. "The first time I tried to serve it to you, you called it rabbit food, but then I said that you were setting a bad example for the girls, not even trying it, so you did, and you couldn't resist. It's my own recipe: mostly oats, maple syrup, and a little bit of coconut."

He raised his eyebrows. "Well, then, how can I say no? Bring it on. But wait a sec, and I'll make some scrambled eggs, too." Then a shadow crossed his face and he tilted his head quizzically.

"I love your scrambled eggs," she reassured him.

He looked like he wanted to ask her something else.

She shrugged, not because she was actually feeling nonchalant, but because she wished she were. "I stayed over a couple of times."

Was it her imagination or did his gaze darken at that?

He ducked before she could say for sure. He came up, forehead wrinkled, hands empty. "Did you move the skillet?"

"In the cabinet next to the stove."

She didn't say, *You put it there. Right before you left. You said it made way more sense for it to be next to the stove.*

He didn't need to be reminded constantly that pieces were missing.

He crossed to the fridge and pulled out the eggs. Broke them into a bowl, added some milk.

He rustled in one of the cabinets and she saw his shoulders rise in tension and fall in defeat.

"Salt and pepper's on the other side," she said quietly.

He shot her a look of gratitude. She wasn't sure if it was purely for the information or for something in the way she'd delivered it.

She'd stayed over twice when the girls were at a sleepover party. And once or twice when they were in the house, because the four of them had been out late or up late here playing board games. And they'd always made sure she woke up in the guest room and he woke up in his room. Which had not always been easy. Once Hunter had snuck upstairs at six a.m. and almost bumped into Clara going to the bathroom.

By that point, she hadn't cared if the girls caught on. She might even have preferred it, because it would have put an end to the sneaking around.

She wondered: If he hadn't lost his memory, would he have come back 100 percent gung ho? Or had there always been a little part of him not completely sure of her, of them?

The thought chilled her.

"How would you feel about the four of us going to Lakeshore Park today?"

She must have startled or made a small noise, because he said, "What?"

"You asked me that. *Before.* We did that. The four of us. That was—it was the first time the four of us all did something together. You texted just like that. 'How would you feel about the four of us going to Lakeshore Park today?'"

"Huh," he said. He cut a pat of butter and let it skate around the bottom of the skillet on the stove.

"I just figured you were feeling nervous about Clara staying with me. At that point, we didn't know each other very well. I mean, you knew Clara spent about half her life at my house, and that Dee and Linda both trusted me enough to have left Clara with me for a couple of days at a time. But I figured you were doubting yourself."

"I guess I might have been."

He hadn't been, though. He'd told her after the fact that the outing was his first attempt to spend time with her, even though he wasn't admitting it to himself yet. She didn't want to tell him that, though. It would be too *leading*. She didn't want him to think she was trying for a do-over.

She wasn't.

She *really, really* wasn't.

Even if she was dying to touch him.

She should say no. There was no way she could go to Lakeshore Park and not think of how it had been the last time around. Tension shimmering in the air between them, nearly from the moment she'd taken off her cover-up and his eyes had looked everywhere except at her skimpy bathing suit.

"I think it would be fun."

Those were not the words she was supposed to have said. Nor was she supposed to be beaming at him. But he was smiling back at her, and God, he hadn't smiled like that since —before. All white teeth and eye crinkles and that almost-dimple and just the sheer ridiculous *glow* of him.

She remembered the first time he'd smiled at her like that. The day they'd gone to Lakeshore.

Even though she knew what mistakes she wasn't supposed to make again, she kept wanting to make them.

"Do you want to go somewhere other than Lakeshore? Because we've already done that?"

She shook her head. Apparently she was going to under-
mine all her own best intentions today.

"It's a little frustrating," he admitted. "I have a brilliant
idea, and it's already old and busted." He wet his hand under
the tap and flicked a few drops of water into the skillet, where
they sizzled. He poured the eggs in and didn't make eye
contact.

"It's different this time, anyway," she said. "Everything's
different."

And she didn't just mean in the bad ways. She didn't just
mean what he'd forgotten and what she'd lost. She meant it
in good ways, too. After spending five days working with him
on the tree house, she didn't see him quite the same way
anymore. He wasn't just the same Hunter she'd left behind,
only minus his memories of her. He was—he was different.
Harder, with something defensive in the set of his jaw. But
also softer, a different, more vulnerable, man than he'd let
her see before.

The man who'd given himself up so thoroughly in those
moments in the dark . . .

No, this visit to Lakeshore would in many ways bear no
resemblance to their first. It was impossible, now, for her to
look at him and see the same remote, self-contained man—
Clara's father—she'd once seen. She knew him too well,
knew all the soft and tender spots under his strong and
leathery surface.

It was harder for her to protect herself from this man.

IT DIDN'T OCCUR to him immediately that this ou
involve Trina in a bathing suit. He'd asked her tota.
neously, because he needed a day's break from tr
work, because the sun was shining brightly outside, ᴗecause
he didn't want his and Clara's time with her to just end,
without fanfare. He wanted to create an experience they'd
remember, distinctly.

If he were honest with himself, he'd say he wanted to
create an experience Trina would remember, too.

But the bathing suit wasn't on his mind.

They'd finished eating the scrambled eggs and fucking
awesome granola and were doing the dishes, bumping
elbows and accidentally twining soapy fingers under the
water, when he suddenly realized that he'd just arranged for
himself to spend an entire day in the presence of her mostly
naked curves. And that it might be a form of beautiful
torture.

Not an hour went by that he didn't think about the night
he'd woken in the middle of kissing her, or that other
encounter, the one he might or might not have dreamed. And
working side by side with her this week, leaning closer to
show her a technique, or squatting beside her to examine one
of the treasures she'd scavenged, it had been increasingly
difficult to keep his hands off her. But he'd successfully suffocated his cravings in hard work. He'd kept his hands to
himself and the thoughts in the dark quiet of his own mind.
Because he would *not* do to her what he'd done to Dee. He
wouldn't let lust lead them both into a trap. If there was no
way, now, to fix what had gone wrong with Dee, he would
make sure Trina didn't make the same mistake with him.

After breakfast, he'd gone upstairs to shower and change,

and it had been then, standing under the water, running his soapy palm across his chest, that it occurred to him to wonder where his bathing suit was.

They would wear bathing suits, of course.

She would wear a bathing suit.

Trina. Bathing suit.

Damn.

His skin buzzed with a low-level anticipation that wouldn't rinse away.

He wondered if this was old territory. If after he'd texted her and invited her to the base's lakefront park the first time, he'd pondered—with a little too much anticipation and a suspicious dryness of the mouth—just exactly what she'd look like, blond hair streaming and shining in the sun, skin bared.

He was getting hard.

He reminded his body that all they were doing was driving to a pretty spot for a picnic and some swimming, but that didn't seem to help with how tight he was strung.

So he made himself think of a fight he'd had once, with Dee. She'd had a new bathing suit and he hadn't even noticed. She'd cried and said he didn't see her anymore, not like *that.* And he'd denied and soothed, but when she'd stopped crying and they'd moved on to other things, he'd felt dirty, like he'd lied. Because the truth was, he knew exactly what she meant and *she was right.* He *didn't* see her anymore, not like that.

That was the flip side of this moment. If he let his mind run away with fantasies about Trina—if he acted on his impulses where she was concerned—they would end up like that. Hurt. Bitter. Dirty.

His head and chest ached. But the truth was, using thoughts of Dee to push away his feelings for Trina just wasn't working as well as it had.

Sometimes it felt like the old Hunter, the one who'd been reckless enough to let himself go with Trina, was trying to break free, and the new Hunter, the cautious, sensible one who wanted to keep her out of harm's way, was losing the battle.

He flung the curtain aside, toweled himself off hard, and rushed himself through dressing, so the fantasies wouldn't have time to re-gather.

Or the memories, if that's what they were.

In the car, the girls were chatty and lighthearted, Trina laughing at their jokes, and it was impossible not to be drawn in. The girls helped, without being asked, to trek the chairs and towels and inflatables they'd picked up at Walmart en route to the beach, and then they flung their cover-ups off and ran pell-mell for the sparkle of the lake.

He tried not to watch out of the corner of his eye as Trina shed her flirty pink cover-up. That stupid barely-there garment had really only made things worse by clinging to her curves and hinting at everything underneath it. Or—well, that was what he'd thought until she took it off.

"Race you to the middle!"

She took off on the inflatable raft, paddling with her hands, and he launched his raft and followed.

Sure. Good idea. You paddle, and I'll try not to ogle you. It took superhuman effort. When he was behind her, he couldn't keep his eyes off the dimples at the base of her spine, or the beginnings of the thoroughly squeezable ass that disappeared into her bikini bottom. And it only got worse when he paddled harder and caught up, because then he had to try really hard to drag his eyes away from the juicy fullness of her breasts spilling over the not-even-particularly tiny bikini top.

Now here they were, floating in the middle of the lake, and he kept sneaking looks at her in that red bikini and then wishing he hadn't. The long, smooth slope of her belly, the dip of her navel, the porcelain of her skin. The squeezable, edible, oh-so-fucking-soft-looking thighs . . . His swim trunks were doing a lousy job of masking his interest.

Not for you, dude.

His body didn't give a shit about that kind of logic.

He cast another sideways look at her, her eyes closed against the brilliant sun overhead. She looked—peaceful. Happy. For the first time since he'd come home.

And the thirteen-year-old boy in him—or maybe the old Hunter—just had to do it. Had to grab the edge of her float, tip her up, and dump her in the water.

She emerged choking and sputtering from the water, her hair plastered to her face. "Bastard!"

She threw herself on him—which of course must have been his subconscious intention all along. He recognized that as soon as her skin—cool on the surface, but he could feel the heat underneath—slipped along his, satiny and wet. Her breasts were alluringly close to his face; if he sat up and dipped his head, he could have that smooth, wet skin against his lips.

But suddenly he was frozen by a question.

"Did I tip you? Last time we came here?"

He said it low, close to her ear. He didn't want the girls to hear, because even though they'd paddled off a good distance now, the water carried sound across its surface. They'd taken the news of his lost memory pretty well in stride. *You don't remember anything?* they'd demanded, and *Will it come back?* but even Clara hadn't freaked out too badly. He'd never reveal to her how scared *he* was by the crevasses in his mind.

Trina paused in her efforts. "No. You were apparently far less of an asshole before."

But she was grinning, and she resumed her project of trying to get more of her body on his raft, more of her weight onto him, and it felt so unfuckingbelievably hot, the contact with her skin, the slip and slide of it, the jiggle and bounce of her, that when she called out, "Girls! I need some help here!" he had to flip himself off the raft and into the water before they could come to her aid, because he wasn't decent viewing with his trunks waving at the sky.

He felt the flit of her body against his in the water, like a lake creature brushing by in the depths. Just the silk of her leg against his, and then she was gone, but he knew it would be a while before he could haul himself back onto the raft.

She pulled herself out of the water, glistening all over.

The cold water had done its work and he was able to dredge himself out of the lake and settle on the raft again.

She reached a hand out and indicated the angry, red scar that marred his torso on the right side. Her fingers didn't even brush him, but he felt the air move over his wet skin, and his whole body tightened. *God.*

"Ugly, huh?"

She shook her head. "It's not ugly. It's a sign that you lived. It could never be ugly to me."

He was not a sentimental man—or at least he never had been, *before.* The self he remembered would have shrugged something like that off, like a pitcher shaking off a catcher's signals. But he knew she meant it, that she was just telling the truth, without any calculation. And he needed to hear it and needed it to be true. So when she reached out her hand again, her fingertips floating over the evidence of his survival, he squeezed it briefly before he let it go.

12

They grabbed Red Robin burgers on the way home, made the girls take showers, and tucked them, fragrant with shampoo and dopey from the sun and activity, into bed.

Since Hunter's return home, they'd been taking turns saying good night to the girls—Trina first, and then Hunter. But tonight, he didn't wait for her to be finished before he came in. While she was sitting on the lower bunk, reminding Phoebe in a low voice how proud she was of her, how lucky she felt to be her mother, Hunter climbed the ladder so his head poked over the upper railing, and she heard his low voice murmuring similarly to Clara.

She shouldn't read anything into it. He'd just chosen to streamline the process tonight.

But it felt cozy. Homey.

It felt like something she'd imagined during his absence, something she'd dreamt up before her hopes and expectations had gotten dashed.

Like the squeeze of his hand over hers this afternoon.

Like the flashes of heat in his eyes, the all-too-familiar way his gaze had settled, heavy, on her half-bare breasts.

Hope had bloomed.

"That was a fun day," Phoebe whispered.

Trina loved bedtime. Because no matter how much of an adolescent her daughter had become during the day, at bedtime she was a child again, trusting, innocent, confiding. "It was, wasn't it?"

"Do you think we'll do stuff like that with Daddy?"

Would they? She didn't know. If Stefan took an interest in them that was more than a passing fancy. If he didn't find that they cramped his style.

Her stomach hurt a little bit at the thought. Because she could hold her own feelings in check and keep herself from getting hurt again, but the idea of Phoebe's disappointment was more than she could bear.

"I don't know, hon," she said. "I hope so. I think so. But Daddy—he's very busy. So we'll see. But I'll do cool things with you." She leaned down and touched her lips to her daughter's smooth forehead. "I love you, Phoebs."

"How much?"

"A bazillion, two gigahertz, and a partridge in a pear tree."

"I love you a bazillion, two gigahertz, and *two* partridges in a pear tree."

Hunter, who had descended the ladder, crossed behind her. His body didn't touch hers, but she could feel the energy and heat of it, and her body hummed in response; she wondered if he could feel it. She wondered whether he'd meant any of it—her hand in his, the way he'd heated her skin with a glance.

"Hey, Phoebe. I had a good time with you today. I'm sorry

I don't remember the last time we hung out, but I'm glad we got another chance."

Trina's heart squeezed. Today—as he'd always been—Hunter had been easygoing with Phoebe, funny and noncommittal, and her usually shy daughter had opened up to him. There had been only a few moments—and if she didn't know him so well, she might not even have noted them—when she saw him fall, for just a split second, into the darkness of forgetting.

In one of those moments, he'd looked to Trina and she'd smiled to tell him it was okay, and she'd seen relief overcome panic. And been absurdly touched by the fact that her presence soothed him. Before she'd remembered that it didn't, couldn't, matter.

"Me, too." Phoebe's voice was small but pleased.

"Good night, kiddo."

He hesitated in the doorway, and his eyes snagged hers, dark and serious. "Good night, Trina." Something in the weave of his gaze and voice left her breathless.

"Good night, Hunter."

He went out, his fingers wrapping the edge of the doorframe, and whether the gesture was deliberate or not, she felt as if he'd let that lingering hand drift over her skin.

Oh, you fool, she told herself, as if that would help. As if it would make the way she felt go away, when nothing would, except time and distance and, eventually, forgetting.

She was envious of his forgetting, she realized.

She climbed the bunk ladder and peeked over the top at Clara, who had drawn her quilt up to her chin.

"Did it work okay?" she whispered. "With the tampons today?"

They'd had an awkward but fruitful lesson on the topic earlier; a tearful Clara had declared that she would never, ever, ever get it to work, but ultimately emerged triumphant from the bathroom and thrown her arms around Trina, whose chest had felt full to overflowing.

"Mmm-hmm," Clara murmured.

"Good. 'Night, Clara." She settled a kiss on the girl's forehead, just as she had done to her own daughter. "I love you, hon."

But before she could retreat down the ladder, Clara reached out and grasped Trina's wrist. "Wait. Don't go."

Trina leaned in close, thinking Clara had something she wanted to ask. Or say. But Clara only held on tight to Trina's wrist, and tears filled Trina's eyes as she realized what Clara was saying. *Don't go. Don't go away. Don't leave me. Don't leave us.*

"Sweetie. I have a couple more days. And we'll visit."

But as she said it, she knew it was not nearly enough, not with all Clara had lost.

"It's not the same. It's not the same. Don't go."

"Oh, baby," said Trina, and rested her head beside Clara's on the pillow. "I love you. I wish I could stay." It felt like her chest was bursting open, like her heart was breaking into a million pieces. For herself, and for Clara, who had lost a mother and was losing another.

What a muddle.

She blinked back tears.

Clara's lids were heavy, and her grip on Trina's wrist had begun to slacken. But the vise around Trina's heart had only tightened.

This. This is what I want, she thought, watching as Clara's last long blink turned to a sigh and sleep.

I'm sorry.

It was Hunter's voice, when he'd told her he couldn't—or wouldn't—try to find his way back to her.

It was her own voice, telling Clara she would never have let her love her like a mother if she'd known it wasn't for keeps.

It was the small voice in her own head, reckoning with all the things she wanted and couldn't have.

This. This is what you get for wanting.

13

She lay in bed, unable to sleep.

She couldn't stop thinking—of these last few days and how good they'd been, the rhythms of being with the girls, watching Hunter in his element, strong and fierce, the four of them working on a project as a—

Not a family!

What was she supposed to think? Today had been—it had been unmistakably *something*. Some progress toward—

Toward what, exactly? She was leaving Saturday. And thank God she was, because she didn't seem to have the slightest ability to keep her head on straight where Hunter was concerned. She kept getting mushy and flirty and hopeful, and she could only be headed toward a fall.

It had probably been a terrible mistake to offer to stay because of Clara's period. She should have just—

But she didn't see how she could have done otherwise. She wouldn't have been able to forgive herself for it.

Her body felt it before her ears heard it or her mind registered it—Hunter's cry from upstairs.

She wouldn't go.

He was a grown man. He could take care of himself.

She was a grown woman. She had to take care of herself —her sanity, her pride, her heart.

The cry came again, low and tortured.

She'd go upstairs. Shake him awake. If he tried to grab her, touch her—if he tried *anything*—she'd put an immediate end to it.

She found herself standing beside her bed. She found herself at the door of her room. She found herself in the hallway, down the hallway, at the bottom of the stairs.

She might not have any skill for pretending with Hunter, but she knew she was pretending to herself. She was pretending that there was any chance that she could resist him. She was pretending that her plan was to stop him if he tried. She was pretending that pride had the slightest chance of winning out over what she felt in his arms.

She found herself outside his bedroom.

She found herself inside the door, at the side of his bed.

She didn't wait for him to grab her or touch her or kiss her. She lay down beside him and kissed him. For the worst of all reasons. Because she wanted it more than she cared about anything else.

She kissed him and kissed him, loving the way he roused under her and groaned, the way he reached for her without hesitation. His tongue slick and alive, his fingers gripping her arms, sliding down to grasp her backside, pulling her close.

She wanted him to stay asleep so she could go with him into whatever he was dreaming, to that place where he remembered and wanted, where they shared a history.

But of course, this time he woke up.

"I didn't dream it the other night." His voice was rough and fuzzy with sleep.

"No," she said. "It wasn't a dream."

She couldn't see him well in the dark, but she could tell that his eyes were on her face. He'd loosened his grip on her, but he hadn't pushed her away or tried to extricate himself. She could feel the length of his erection wedged between them, and she had to exert conscious effort not to wriggle against it. Not to rock her hips. She wondered what would happen if she did. If he would press back or stop her. Would it be night rules, or day rules?

"Did you really think it was a dream?"

"No."

"But you pretended you did."

"I didn't really *know*. I suspected it wasn't. But there's no really good way to ask a woman if you actually—"

There was a smile in his voice now.

"Guess not," she admitted.

There was something she wanted to know. And if she asked it, everything would change, one way or another. One of the dreams she'd held onto for too long would fall away, and *she* would be wide awake.

She asked it anyway, because it was night. Because she could feel him trying not to move against her the same way she was trying not to move against him, could feel what it cost him in held breath and taut muscle. Because it might be her last chance to talk to this half-awake part of him that remembered her.

"Did you *want* it to be a dream?"

He got very still under her, so still she could feel the slight throb of blood in the thick vein that ran the length of him, the slight involuntary clench of internal muscle—his body trying to assert itself against his better judgment.

She'd almost despaired of an answer by the time he spoke. She'd readied herself to stand, to pull away, to lose the heat and familiarity of him.

To say goodbye to the dream where they could still meet.

And then he said it.

"No."

HE'D WOKEN up with her tongue in his mouth and he'd thought, *Hell, yeah,* and then, *Oh, wow, this is going to keep happening, isn't it?* And it had felt as good as a dream, the softness and strength of her body on his, how her kiss begged him, those almost-noises she made in the back of her throat.

He could have stopped, then, but he couldn't have, either.

This is bigger than my mind.

He followed the dream of her where it took him.

My body remembers.

She'd gotten him so hard. And not just that. She'd roused all of him, body and lost shards of memory, something as deep as soul, and he was still vibrating at that fever pitch, like the slightest touch, or even a command from her, could take him over the edge. And he wanted it, the flesh weak at this vulnerable hour. He wanted to throw caution and good sense and his protectiveness of her feelings to the fucking wind and finish what she'd started.

He could smell her, rich and salty.

He wanted her, a craving so sharp and bad it was in his bones and fingernails.

Fuck.

Did you want it to be a dream? she'd asked.

And he'd told her the absolute, complete, unequivocal truth.

No.

She sighed after his revelation, and for a moment—a ridiculously hopeful moment—he thought she was about to kiss him again. But then she slipped off him and sat beside him on the bed. She reached for the light and left them blinking, like vulnerable night creatures exposed to day.

"I can't do this," she said. "I can't wake up again tomorrow morning and pretend nothing happened. It—it *hurts.* And I know it's not your fault. It's my fault. But I—I can't. So I'm sorry. For being confusing and sending mixed messages, but I have to go."

She stood up, but without thinking at all about it, he reached for her hand, held her fast.

"Wait."

Her eyes were big, with bruised shadows beneath. Her mouth soft and red and kissed. She looked scared and uncertain. She looked like he felt.

He could keep this safe for both of them. He could let her walk out of here without ever asking her all the questions that crowded his mind.

He knew that was what he should do. He should leave it alone. But he couldn't, any more than she'd been able to when she'd asked him her question. Something had shifted today. When they'd played and teased in the water. When she'd reached for his scar. When she'd looked at him so tenderly and told him there was no ugliness in him.

"Was it always—like this?" he asked.

It was a relief to speak the words aloud. As if he'd been holding the question back ever since that first time he'd woken to her.

"Like this?"

"This good."

She tried not to smile at that, but he saw the hint of it. "Yes."

"So we did have sex. Before."

"Oh, yes."

Now she looked at him. Now she let him see the heat and longing. "And you tried resisting it last time, too."

He nodded. That made perfect sense to him. That he would be consistent across the gulf of his lost self.

"But you wanted it to happen?"

Her face was still mostly hidden, the half-light adding a veil. "No. Not at first. Because of the girls. Because if they'd found out, and then things hadn't worked out, it would have been hard for them, and I didn't think it was worth risking that. And because of Dee."

It was the first time she'd said Dee's name, at least in his available memory.

"Because it felt like taking something that was hers."

She and Dee had connected because of the girls, but over time, waves and smiles at pickup and drop-off had morphed into coffee and confessions. For Dee, at least, he knew it had been a significant friendship. He could imagine how crossing that line, even after death, might feel very wrong.

"But we—we did. We did it anyway."

She nodded.

"And it was—good?"

Some memory lit behind her face, a half-smile, and she

was twice as beautiful. "It was amazing. And we both said—we both said it wasn't like anything else. I kept trying to make analogies with food. Like if you'd only ever had orange juice from concentrate and then someone squeezes you a glass at the table. And you were like, *That other thing? That wasn't even orange juice.* Or chocolate. We actually had sort of a fight about chocolate, because I said it was like if you'd been eating only grocery-store milk chocolate and then you discovered, I don't know, Ghirardelli dark chocolate or something, you'd be like, *That thing? Wasn't even chocolate.* But you said that for s'mores the grocery-store stuff was actually better because it tasted like childhood. And we argued about it. Not really arguing. Kidding around. I said if you still thought you wanted that grocery-store stuff after you'd had real chocolate, maybe you hadn't just come as hard as I had—"

She was smiling. Grinning, absolutely beautiful with her eyes all alight and the joy shining under her skin. Lost in the story she was remembering, and *God,* he wanted to be there with her, *so bad.* Where she'd gone, into their history, what she was seeing, what she was feeling—he wanted it. And he felt so howlingly lonely all of a sudden, a breaking in two that he couldn't bear for a second.

She suddenly seemed to recall herself. Stiffened, her expression closing down. "I'm sorry." She turned away. "I don't think this is a good idea."

But it wasn't like that. Not something at a distance from him. True, he couldn't remember. But—

It felt like his story, too. And for the first time, he *wanted it to be his story.*

The realization terrified him. He had *no right.* No right to raise her hopes.

"I don't blame you for that," he said. "Not at all. You've gotten jerked around enough."

She started to get up from the bed. But then she hesitated. "Why did you ask that question?"

He knew she was referring to when he'd asked if it had been good between them.

"To satisfy curiosity? To help you get your memory back?"

He understood what she was asking. And how all of these questions had been leading them, even in the dark, toward an answer. Toward the only possible answer.

"No," he said. "No. I need—I want to know what happened. I want to know what I felt, because—"

Her gaze scraped over his face, left him raw, like she'd looked and seen everything there was to see and taken away the last of his protective shell. But the converse, too. Like he'd taken away the last of hers. The two of them utterly naked, all pale, thin skin.

"I think I might be starting to feel that way again."

14

It was so little, and so late. Today was Wednesday and she was leaving Saturday, and there was no way—*no way*—she would change her plans—and Phoebe's—because of a scrap, a wisp, not even a declaration.

It was so little. So very little. Not a promise at all.

"I'm leaving. Saturday."

He nodded. "I have no right to ask anything of you."

"I can't change my plans. Phoebe—"

She couldn't even finish the sentence. She wouldn't put Phoebe through another upheaval, not for anything.

"I know."

But he *wanted* to try.

And she wanted to let him.

As bruised as she felt, as battered, there was still a tight knot of hope somewhere deep down inside her.

Memory was a bitch in this case. Because she remembered that last year, it had been a little like this. He'd been scheduled to leave and they'd been sliding down a slope together, the descent gathering speed, and she'd had a feeling that there was a landslide under them. And then that very last night, which easily could have turned out to be nothing more than *goodbye,* had instead been new firm ground.

Memory wouldn't let her give up hope that that could happen again. Treacherous, tempting memory.

If she told him more about what had happened between them, she would have to relive it all.

All the firsts, not just with him, but in her life.

She'd have to make herself completely vulnerable *yet again,* unfurl her longings and hope that his would grow to match hers.

And yet: if there was a chance that remembering for him could help him get there, didn't she need to give him that?

Even more: if there was a chance she could have him back, didn't she have to take it? Because under all the fear was how much she missed him. Missed *them.*

There really was no choice here for her. There was only what had to be done, and whatever she could do to protect herself from it.

She took a deep breath. "It started when Clara told Phoebe what was going on with your mom and Ray. That your mom was going to move to California and couldn't take Clara with her."

The gratitude she saw on his face—it shamed her. That she'd considered holding this back from him, when it *was* his. Not hers to keep.

"Did I get mad at my mom when she did that?"

Trina hesitated a moment, wondering if she had any responsibility to try to keep this recounting from going down like *Groundhog Day.* "Do you want me to tell you what you did? Or what I think you *wish* you did?"

He laughed, so many white teeth in his naturally tan face. "Good point. Okay. So, I flipped out, huh?"

"Well, understandably—you were three months from deployment and she was completely upending your childcare plans. Or so you told me afterward. I wasn't actually around for the mushroom cloud. You showed up to grab Clara from a playdate with Phoebs and you looked like you were going to vibrate out of your skin, so I asked what was wrong, and you told me."

"And you just, what—just offered to take her?"

"No. My first thought was actually, holy shit, I hope he's not hinting that *I* should take her. But you weren't. At least I don't think you were. You were just venting. And it was kind of nice—it was the first time we'd ever really had much of a conversation. You'd always seemed very—remote—"

"Oh, that's flattering." He made a face at her, and she felt herself smiling, almost against her will.

"I don't mean it in a bad way. Soldierly. Self-possessed, self-contained—"

"I'm still not getting the warm fuzzies."

She smirked. "Well, sorry. But you're not the easiest guy to get to know. I'm not going to lie about that. After that day, we were kind of friends. But it was actually Clara who hinted that I should take her."

"She *what*?"

"Yeah, you were mad at her the first time, too." She laughed. "At least you're consistent."

"So, what, she *invited herself*?"

The expression on his face matched exactly the one he'd

worn the last time he'd uttered those words to her. A weird, not unpleasant, sense of déjà vu settled over her.

"She was nervous. You were considering sending her to stay with her aunt and uncle and cousin Peter. And apparently cousin Peter is sort of like cousin Dudley in the Harry Potter books? But maybe with some strange adolescent lusting thrown in for good measure?"

He looked like he'd been struck. "I didn't—"

"You didn't know until Clara told me. And then I told you. Which put a temporary end to our conversation because you had to go have a heart-to-heart with your sister and brother-in-law."

"Well, thank you for saving me from doing *that* all over again," he said.

This time, they smiled at each other at the same moment, then looked away.

"The next time I saw you, I said, 'You know, it wouldn't be such a big deal for Clara to stay with us. The girls go to the same school; they're in most of the same activities; and Clara's not exactly high maintenance. Dee's left her with me for a week at a time, and Linda for several days at a time, so Clara will be comfortable, and you can trust that I know what I'm doing.'"

"And I said, 'Don't be ridiculous, I can't ask you to do that.'"

"You used literally those exact words."

"And you said—" He screwed up his face as if trying to remember. "'No, really, it's not a big deal. I think it would be fun.'"

She had. Almost to the word. "Do you re—"

"No. Or, not consciously. I just, I don't know, kind of let my mind go blank, and based on what I know of you, thought about what I imagined you'd say."

"That's a little—freaky."

"Not as freaky as—" He hesitated. "In the dark—"

Her body was shot through with anticipatory tingles.

"—I know you."

His words—the way they rippled under her skin—forced a low, small sound from her, and his eyes darkened.

"It's like a dream or something. Like returning to a dream I've had before, and starting up in the same place again. But if I wake up all the way ..."

He wouldn't quite meet her eye, and disappointment settled on her like a cloak. This—this was what she'd feared. "You wake up and wish you hadn't done it."

He looked up at her, startled.

"I didn't say *that,* did I?" he asked.

"No."

"Because I don't. Wish I hadn't done it, I mean."

He watched her, quietly for a moment, and she could almost feel the weight of his gaze on her skin. And then he said, "Come here."

IN THE LAMPLIGHT she was even more beautiful than she'd been by day, and he drew her close slowly, not wanting to rush the moment. For a long time he just hovered his mouth over hers, feeling her breath, smelling her skin, glorying in the way she reached for him without even moving. He kissed her lower lip first, then the upper, then her whole mouth, but gently, not asking her to open yet, even though he'd just had so much more. Because this was different—the lights were on, he was wide awake, and the rules he'd been following moments earlier no longer held.

And if she'd responded to the wild passion of their middle-of-the-night encounter, this was even better. She shivered and shifted at the light touch, and a sweet little whimper broke free from her and rattled around in his chest.

But then she stopped the kiss and frowned at him.

"What?"

"That wasn't how you kissed me the other first time."

The other first time. Funny that this felt like a first kiss to both of them, despite everything that had already passed between them.

"No? How did I do it?"

"You held my face. Like this."

She reached for his hands and laid them against her skin, creamy and warm.

"And you looked at me for a long time. Your eyes were really dark and you kept staring, and I just looked back at you, and it was the hottest thing ever."

"Yeah?"

"Yeah."

Her eyes were a bright blue that possibly didn't exist anywhere else in nature, some gray in them, some purple. He could imagine he'd wanted to stare into them for a good long time, but it wasn't really her eyes that had his attention right now. It was all the other details of her face—the fine pale arch of her eyebrows, the bright blush of her cheeks, the way her lips parted as he stared, the lower one begging to be bitten.

"And then what did I do?"

"You kissed the shit out of me."

"Oh?" He raised an eyebrow.

"It had been a long time coming. We'd already had a few *We can't, we shouldn't* conversations. The tension was —insane."

"Yeah?" Because the tension was pretty insane for him right now. Like something strung tight and set to vibrate, just behind his breastbone.

She nodded and bit her lower lip. *Oh, hey.* He wanted to be the one biting that lip.

"You want me to do it that way again? Just like the first time?"

He was expecting her to say yes, and he would have obliged her, but surprisingly, she shook her head *no.* "No. I want you to do it the way you were doing it just now. Light like that. You've never done that before, and—"

Her face was still in his hands, and he *did* want to kiss the shit out of her, but she was telling him something. Something important.

"—I like that it's new for both of us."

She said it shyly. Like she wasn't sure, despite that kiss, if they were really doing this.

And they shouldn't. They shouldn't be doing this. Every line he crossed, every line he tugged her over, he risked hurting her.

But *oh my God* the way she was looking at him. Expectantly. Eagerly. And oddly fearlessly. As if she'd passed beyond all her reservations.

This must have been what it was like. Last time.

And he had the quickest flash—memory? Fantasy?—of her upturned face and her eyes locked on his and the feel of her mouth opening, yielding, under his, and his body thrummed, hard, and he knew he was going to kiss her again, no matter how bad an idea it was.

He leaned close and touched her mouth lightly with his again, and her mouth and the air around them and his fingertips and his whole fucking *body* buzzed with the power of it. She was trembling and electric and one part of him wanted to wrap her up and hold her tight, strap her down, even, to control the high-tension-wire sizzle. The other part of him wanted to spend all night doing exactly what he was doing right now, brushing his mouth back and forth across hers, hearing her breath catch and lurch and sigh out of her, feeling that same breath like a touch on his skin.

How long could they do this? Sit here half-kissing, a touch so light it woke up every baby hair and sleepy nerve ending, a touch that without pressure or tickle or purposefulness felt like it had traveled across the whole surface of his skin? He was impatient for more at the same time he never wanted it to stop.

She tilted her head up so his mouth slid down her jaw, down her throat, and—when she didn't stop him—to where the curve of her breasts flared.

"It's all backwards," she said breathlessly. "A year ago, you had sex with me. Last week, you made me come."

Hearing her say it, the frankness of it, got him the rest of the way to stupidly hard.

"And now you're—"

His lips brushed back and forth just above the lace edge of her nightgown, silencing her.

He didn't know what they were doing. There were so many things he didn't know—who he was, who she was, what had happened, what would happen. But there were things he did know, too. The scent of her skin, here, where lace teased curves. The satin feel of it. The hitch in her breath. And so much more he wanted to know.

"Now," he said, "I'm getting to know you."

15

She'd thought she'd known him. She'd thought she'd remembered. But she hadn't known anything.

Now she was getting to know his mouth. His lips were soft, gentle, then, suddenly, commanding. His tongue sought her. The barest touch against her lips, a ghost drifting by. A slick shift against hers, raising every downy hair on her body. A thrust that told her he wasn't going to hold back when they were naked, her legs spread for him. A tease against her upper lip that made her want to push him down between her thighs and open herself to his kiss.

His breath moved in her hair, against the shell of her ear, the hypersensitive skin where neck met shoulder. It sped when her body arched and curved under his, when she moaned with involuntary pleasure, when she pressed her hips against his erection.

He whispered, cajoled, commanded, teased. *Just like that, sexy. Oh, God, I love it when you make that noise. Love it. Oh. Oh. Do that again,* he begged, when her fingers slipped into his briefs and wrapped briefly around him and her thumb slicked pre-cum over the head of his cock. *Does that feel good?* he demanded, when his erection settled right at the juncture of her thighs and he moved, so carefully over the cloth there, the friction hard enough to drive her mad but not hard enough to burn. *You want more? Faster? Or how about this? Slower? Yeah? You like that?*

His biceps bunched when he rose on his arms above her. The position brought out his pecs and the cords in his neck and forearms. The look on his face was full of wonder and awe.

She had never known how many ways there were to kiss. Hundreds. Thousands. Softer. Harder. Faster. Slower. Just the corner, just this lip, just the tip, mouths falling open so wide, so deep, you could fall in, you could drown, you could swallow each other up. Teasing, inviting, yielding, giving up, giving in, throwing yourself away, getting lost, coming back and rising up and rolling over and being in charge, first him, then her, then him again, because she loved that, his weight on her, the bossiness of his kisses, the demand of his hands on her body, the insistence of his cock against her belly.

God. God, God, *God.*

Does it feel good? Can I make it feel better?

She learned everything about his cock, the heat, the softness of the skin, the way velvet clung to steel. She cupped a hand over the cut head, smooth as silk from how tight the skin stretched. She gloried in the slickness, the heft, the taste of him against her tongue when she ducked down. He brought her back up to lick the taste of himself from her mouth. He rolled against her, first top to bottom, then side to side, like he couldn't get enough, his breath panting hard now, his pupils blown wide and dark.

A flush rose in his face. His rhythm went ragged. He made a soft sound, another, a growl, a groan. He said, *kiss me again, keep kissing me, if you keep doing that I'm going to come, are you?*

She kissed him and kissed him and kissed him. That was all it took. That and the way their bodies sought each other, through all the layers of clothes, through all the wrong turns and folds of time and memory.

She recognized, long before he made the last thrust against her, long before his face contorted with it, before she cried out with it, before he tucked his head into her neck and lay spent and wrecked beside her, that this would be the first time. That even though he'd laid her bare, even though in the dark only days ago he'd taken her apart, even though he'd watched her lose herself in pleasure before, this was the first time, the only time. And that sense of wonder you can only have once—*look what he did. Look what* we *did. Look—*

That was how it felt. Like it had never happened before.

And it hadn't. She'd never been taken apart so far she couldn't be put back together again. This was the first time.

16

"Hunter. Hunter!"

She was shaking him.

"I'm awake. I'm awake." His mouth was dry, his heart pounding. In his mind's eye, the dream was still sharp in all his senses. The oppressive, looming dark, the ache in his lungs from breathing the fine particles of dust, and—as he tried to clear his way through—those eyes peering from the blackness, shocked and accusing.

Light came through between the blinds and the windows. Morning.

"Hunter, what is it?"

"I think I—I think I remember something."

"You don't think it was just a dream?"

"No. It was a memory."

And, just beyond the dream, his mind knew there was something more to see and know, something crucial.

Something terrible.

What had the doctor said?

It's also possible to have some retrograde amnesia even in response to psychological trauma. I'm sure you've heard of child-hood abuse victims or even adult rape victims with no memory of the incident?

For all this time, since coming home to Trina, he'd wanted to remember the missing pieces. At first for his own benefit, because the lost time felt like a wounded place in his psyche. Then, last night, he'd wanted to remember so he could give himself back to her, whole. But now, suddenly, he wondered.

Did he want to know everything that was missing?

What if, in that gap between past and present, there was something he'd been so unable to grapple with that he'd chosen to elide it?

What would seeing it do to him?

What would it do to what lay between him and Trina?

"Hunter," she whispered.

As his eyes adjusted to the light, he could see her a little bit, and the fear on her face reflected the fear that had suddenly sprung up in his heart.

"What is it?"

"I don't know," he admitted. "There was a building. It was supposed to be empty. But—it wasn't empty. There was someone in it. And something terrible was about to happen."

Her eyes were wide, startled. He'd frightened her. Not, he thought, with his words. He'd infected her with his own fear.

"But that could be any dream. Right? No reason to think it was a memory."

He couldn't explain why this felt different, why it felt—real. Why it felt like the truth, an unwanted truth. There was something, a dark shape, forming from the dread in his belly, like a golem forming out of riverbank mud, and it would rise and come for him. He knew that, now. And—

"Do you want to talk about it?"

"No."

If there was something there, and it was destined to surface, it would have the power to change who he was, just as he'd been changed by the discovery that he'd forgotten Trina and all she'd meant to him. And what men saw during war did alter them forever, he knew that well.

If he remembered . . . if it changed who he was, changed what he believed—

"Hunter."

She was calling to him. Trying to call him out of the dark place he'd slipped into. And *God,* he wanted to follow the sound of her voice.

"Talk to me."

"What if—what if the thing I forgot is something I can't live with?"

"Like what?" she asked.

"What if I did something, or didn't do something, and someone died because of it?"

She closed her eyes. "That would be terrible," she said. "But you *would* live with it. You would find a way to live with it."

"What if *you* couldn't live with it?"

"That wouldn't happen."

She sounded so certain. The same way she had when she'd told him his scars could never be ugly to her. He envied her certainty. The ground under his own feet was rutted, potholed, ready to trip him up. Things weren't where he'd put them—neither real things in the real world nor his own thoughts.

"Shh," she said, and kissed him. Her mouth was soft and warm, and the kiss brought back last night. God, she'd been amazing. Her mouth, her hands, her body against his. The sounds she made, how good she'd made him feel.

All he had to do was believe she was right. There was nothing in his head that would trip him up and bring him down. There was nothing ugly hidden in there, waiting to spring out of the dark. There was just Trina, beautiful in the light, and she was looking down at him patiently, waiting for him to come back from the nightmare so he could kiss her again.

He could believe her. He could.

He reached for her, then froze as a creak came from the hall. A door.

"Oh, shit," she said. One of the girls was awake. His eyes found the clock. Six a.m. Probably too early for her to be up for good, but it was possible.

They lay still in the dark as the bathroom door opened and closed. The length of her, the heat of her—he was suddenly aware of his morning wood. He pressed himself against her and she giggled.

The toilet flushed, the bathroom door opened, footsteps receded down the hall, and the girls' door creaked again.

They were undiscovered. For now.

"I should go back downstairs," she said.

"Do you have to?"

"I think—I should, right?"

"Probably. Before the girls wake up."

It was hard to think straight, with his mind still cloudy

from sleep and the nightmare, with her thigh exerting enough pressure against his cock that he didn't think it was accidental. She was leaving Saturday. Or—

Or he would ask her to stay longer.

But he couldn't do that, could he? Couldn't ask her to give up the opportunity to do what she'd always wanted to do. That thing that lit her up when she talked about it. Couldn't ask her to bait-and-switch Phoebe again. Couldn't ask her, not when he literally didn't know his own mind.

She drew away from him, taking the caress of her leg, the heat of her body, with her.

She hesitated with her hand on the edge of the bed, her fingers close enough that if he'd moved his hand just a little, he could grab them.

And then she was gone.

IT WAS hard for her to fall back to sleep. Her bed in the guest room was cold. A hard knot of anxiety formed in her chest. This was exactly what she wasn't supposed to have let happen. She wasn't supposed to let herself want and hope and *have*.

It could be so much worse, now. Because he'd done it knowingly and willingly, and so if he took it away, that would be knowing and willing, too. And it would hurt that much more. And that sure as hell looked like what was happening. Last night, everything between them had been pure, easy, beautiful. And then this morning, he'd been panicked, ready to run away from her.

What the hell was she supposed to do? With two days to go, what the hell made sense? Nothing.

She didn't know which man she'd find when she went downstairs, the one who'd begged for stories and then brought her new, better fantasies to life—or the one who'd woken up panicked.

And she didn't know which man she wanted to find. Maybe it would be easiest if he turned away from her, refused to acknowledge what had happened. Pushed her away and let her go without drawing her in further.

God knew, the further in she got, the harder it would be to walk away.

And she had to walk away. Right?

Unless—

Unless he could give her some certainty. Something like a promise. And she couldn't expect that from a man who was hurt and confused.

Fuck.

She got up, pulled on her clothes, and went out to the kitchen. He was there, frying eggs on an electric griddle. The girls were nowhere in sight.

He raised his gaze and smiled.

Oh, *hell,* she thought, because she'd almost fainted from relief, and that told her how doomed she was. She could lie to herself all she wanted, tell herself it would be better if he pushed her away, but deep down, at the fifty-second level, she knew what she wanted.

"Hello, sleepyhead. Something keep you up late?"

She wanted to glare at him, but all she could do was grin like a schoolgirl.

He looked her over, his eyes lingering over her breasts, where she could feel her nipples tightening under the soft knit. She should have put a bra on. Or not. She liked the color rising in his cheeks. And the way his gaze wouldn't let hers go.

"How do you like your eggs?"

"Over hard."

"I would have said just hard enough. Didn't hear you complaining."

She shot him a glance and found him smirking at her. "Have you been waiting for me to show up so you could make that joke?"

"Just thought of it, actually."

"What would you have said if I'd said 'over easy'?"

He flipped an egg and tipped his head, thinking. "Probably, 'Mmm. Yeah. That's the way I like it, too.'" He loaded the words with innuendo.

She shivered. He probably could have said just about anything in that voice and had the same effect on her. "'Sunny side?'"

He laughed. "'Honey, both sides are your sunny side.'"

"You would *not* have."

And yet, as utterly ridiculous as the words were, the way he was running his eyes over her, the rough edge in his voice —that probably would have worked, too.

"No," he admitted. "I wouldn't have. You just happen to have served me up the best straight line ever." He tossed two pieces of thick-cut ham onto the griddle. "Come here."

She rested her cheek against his chest and let him draw her into a hug, loving the hardness of his body under the softness of the knit shirt. She put her arms around him and stroked his back, pressing her hips against him until she felt him harden.

"Over medium," she said, and his laugh rumbled under her cheek. She could have stayed there all day, but he stepped away to slip the spatula under his eggs and deposit them on plates.

She shivered and wanted him back.

They sat across from each other at the kitchen table. Sunlight streamed in.

"Let's go to Dungeness Spit today," he said.

She laughed.

"No. Don't tell me we did that last time, too."

She nodded.

"Huh," he said. "You know what's crazy? I feel like he—the old me—is a different guy completely. Like he's your ex. And I'm—well, I'm trying to one-up him."

"Um," she said, "you're jealous? Of your old self?"

She was teasing him, but the truth was, she loved the heck out of that. He was *jealous.* Of the last guy who'd had her. Even if he was his own usurper.

That felt big. Real.

Maybe—maybe this would be okay. Maybe they would spend the day together and it would all become clear—to both of them. Maybe they'd get to a place of certainty and at least half-promises, enough that she could call Stefan and tell him she'd changed her mind, she wasn't coming. That's what she'd do: she'd give it today to play out, and then she'd make a decision.

"Yeah. Crazy. Told you. And not exactly jealous. But—I want you to be thinking about *this* me. Not *that* me—"

His voice had softened, and she realized it was a real

confession. On the same scale as the one he'd made last night, that he wanted to feel that way about her again.

The man she'd fallen in love with had been amazing in so many ways. She had admired him and wanted him and imagined a life with him. But this man—

This man was letting her in in a way that man hadn't.

She'd thought she'd opened her heart to the old Hunter, but the new Hunter made her want to lay herself bare in every possible way.

"Oh, *that* guy," she said, putting some flippancy in her voice. "He's totally old news."

She'd caught him off guard and made him smile again, and God, that smile—the lines at the corners of his eyes, the creases in his cheeks that were almost, but not quite, dimples.

Her heart felt like it was going to burst. Yes, she had a really tough decision to make. But not right this second. Right this second, she just wanted to be here. In this kitchen, him asking her to spend the day in the sunshine with him.

"I'd love to go to Dungeness Spit with you."

"In anticipation of your 'yes,' I made sandwiches."

She laughed out loud at that, and he ducked his head. "Let me guess. Not a surprise?"

She shook her head, and he gave her a wry smile in return. It was one of the things she'd fallen for about him. That he didn't assume the care and feeding of the girls was her responsibility. On their Lakeshore Park outing, he'd bought them all lunch at the snack shack. And *before,* he'd often taken responsibility for packing a picnic lunch. She didn't have much of a history of relationships, but she'd heard enough women bitching about their husbands to know that wasn't a thing you could take for granted. And *hell,* after a lifetime of being a single mom, she didn't take much of anything for granted, and he'd been almost too much to absorb. A guy who cooked breakfast. A guy who *made* *sandwiches.*

A towering, built, gorgeous guy who could rock her world in bed *and* do all that.

She looked up to find him watching her.

"What are you thinking about, beautiful?"

"You've—you've never called me that before."

His mouth opened and he stared at her in astonishment. "I knew that other guy was a fucking idiot." He set his fork down and reached across the table to push a strand of hair behind her ear. "You're crazy beautiful."

She lost her breath, the way he was looking at her.

HEY, man. So glad you're okay. We were a little freaked out. And sorry it took me so long to get back to you. Shit's crazy right now. But we'll be home soon! Can't wait to see you and hear about what's been going on. Yeah, I know what happened. I can't believe no one told you. I guess things got chaotic and they were just trying to save your sorry-ass life. Anyway, gist is, we went into a building that was supposed to be empty, it wasn't (goat fuck), full of T-men, brief fire-fight. A grenade took out a corner of the building and there was a haji woman trapped under some rubble. She probably had been using the building for shelter before the insurgents went in and then was too terrified to show herself. You tried to get her out, we tried to talk you out of it, but you were a crazy man, H. No one could get you to stop digging. I mean, you were like in there, fingernails bloody, the whole nine yards. And then there was another explosion. Probably another

grenade. She was killed, you took that piece of rebar in the chest. I'm sorry to be brief, but I gotta run now. Feel free to ask questions if you want. I might not get your email before we're outta here but I'll try to get back to you if I can. Stay safe. Guess that's easier now, huh?

"Hunter?"

He wasn't sure how long he'd been staring at the screen. Just—staring. He'd stopped to check his email before they left for the spit, and here he was, some number of minutes or hours, or for all he knew, days later.

"What is it?" Trina came up behind him and touched his hair. His whole body leapt to life at the touch, despite how wired the email had made him feel.

He pushed his chair back a little, gesturing to her that she should read the screen. She leaned in and skimmed it.

"Oh," she said. "Oh, Hunter."

"I still feel like it's something that happened to someone else, though. I mean, I see the story. I get that she was probably scared, crying. But—the way he described me—I'm not that guy. I'm the weigh-the-consequences, think-it-through, figure-out-a-plan guy. Not the guy who starts digging in the rubble like a madman when his men are telling him to get the hell out."

"You could write back to him. Ask him."

"Do you think he knows?"

"He might."

The pain of it was, *he* knew. Somewhere down in the depths of his mind, he knew what had happened that day. But he couldn't get to it. It was locked behind a wall.

"God," he said quietly. "I hate it. That there's all this stuff in there. Buried. That I can't see. Like it's waiting for me."

"Isn't that kind of true of all of us?" Trina asked. She put her arms around him, pressed her breasts against his back. For a brief moment, the pain and darkness in his head receded.

"What's buried in your head?" he asked.

"Well, I don't know, do I?"

"You know some of it. You must have things you push down."

"I try not to."

"No buried anger?"

She laughed. "Well, plenty of hostility toward Stefan and his limited contributions toward Phoebe's well-being. Twenty-three chromosomes—I guess I should be glad that it was the right number, right? Expensive Christmas gifts that mainly serve to make her notice how not expensive most of mine are. And cash when I beg nicely. But that's hardly buried."

"You don't act bitter."

"I don't want to be bitter. And I don't want her to hear me being bitter. If we're going to make this thing work, we have to go into it with a good attitude."

"Are you excited about it? The job?"

He turned in his chair so he could see her face. He wasn't sure, not anymore, what he wanted her to say.

She bit her lip. "Yes. Of course."

That heavy feeling in his chest—that was disappointment.

"But—there's a part of me that's not sure, either. Whether this is the right thing."

And that was fear.

He didn't want to let her go, but he was terrified of the alternative. Of her staying.

What if—

What if he couldn't—

What if he disappointed her the way he'd—

"I'm afraid he'll let her down. I don't think he'll be very involved. I think she'll be sort of a trophy daughter to him."

So it wasn't that she didn't want to leave him. It was that she didn't trust Stefan Spencer with Phoebe.

"How could anyone make Phoebe just a *trophy*?" he demanded. "She's terrific." For the last week, he'd been teaching Phoebe to use the power tools. She was fearless and full of ideas, wanting to know why things had to be done a certain way, suggesting out-of-the-box alternatives, and then listening intently as he explained why her ideas could—or might not—work. If she were his daughter—

If he'd gotten Trina pregnant, instead of Dee?

Impossible to imagine of course. Impossible to imagine the world without either Clara or Phoebe. But if he'd gotten Trina pregnant, he would have done the right thing by her, just as he had by Dee. And if Phoebe had been his daughter, he never would have let her out of his sight, up and left to live a thousand miles away. And as for the token gifts and making Trina ask for money . . .

He would never have let them go. Never have let them find family in *another man.*

If he'd been her real father.

If he'd been a man who knew himself capable of love.

"Phoebe is terrific." She smirked. "It's my genes."

He laughed, and it snapped him, once again, out of the dark place he'd been tempted to go.

The ground of the spit wasn't smooth and sandy but a mix of slippery seaweed, ankle-slaying stones, and pebbles that slipped and slid underfoot. To either side of them, Puget Sound undulated in their peripheral vision, bringing vertigo in waves.

They'd calculated the tide correctly, which meant that it was still going out, and there was enough beach for walking, but not an abundance of it, and what beach existed was canted ever-so-slightly downward to the left.

She'd forgotten how much being out on the spit felt like being at sea in a boat. She felt unmoored, unprotected—but also utterly thrilled by the wind whipping around her, the ocean air moving in her hair—very much as she imagined a traveler setting out on a long ocean voyage must have felt.

Hunter took her hand. The girls had run on ahead, and then stopped to examine the beach detritus, repeating the pattern again and again to keep their distance from the adults. Which was fine with Trina, who squeezed Hunter's hand tighter and tried to think only of how happy she was in this exact moment in this exact place. If you tucked yourself tight enough into the present, the past and future could go screw.

"So. The infamous first kiss. How did that come about?"

Oh, so they were going there, again. She wanted to ask him what the hell they were doing. What they'd been doing last night, kissing like that, touching like that. What they were doing today, playing at courtship in the face of her departure. What they were *doing*.

But he didn't know the answer any better than she did. She knew that. All she could do was tell the story and *hope*.

"We each, separately, took the girls to the same sleepover party. By that point, we'd had a few charged moments, but we'd agreed nothing was going to happen. For all the afore-mentioned reasons. You were leaving, you didn't do love, it would confuse the shit out of the girls if they found out, blah blah blah. I pulled up to drop off Phoebe, and I saw you there with Clara, and I decided not to get out of the car because I didn't trust myself. I already had enough experience to know that my resolve was nonexistent when it came to you and that no matter how good my logic was, if I got within a couple of feet of you, it was dead. But you came over and leaned down and peeked in the car window. I could feel—"

She hesitated and he turned, his eyes quizzical.

"That buzz, you know?"

"This buzz?"

He stopped walking for long enough to bring his face near hers and sure enough, there was the electric thrum that always leapt between them.

When she drew back, she saw that his eyes had darkened and his lower lip softened. Her body softened, too, an echo.

"It was a warm summer night and probably a full moon or something. It was the kind of night when things happen, whether you want them to or not. And I did. I wanted things to happen. I'd been wanting it day and night for days and days, and—"

She felt heat roll through her at the memory.

"So yeah," she said, recovering the power of speech with some effort. "You leaned down. And all you said was, 'I'm feeling like grabbing some sushi. Wanna come?' I knew I should say no. I sort of even tried to say no. But you convinced me it would just be a quick dinner. I knew what was going to happen, I think. We were both just waiting for a chance to do the wrong thing, but I went anyway. Maybe because it was that kind of night. Where everything is more intense. All your senses. Everything feels like sex. The air is charged and the food is foreplay—you watched me eat like you couldn't take your eyes off my mouth, and I've *never* thought sushi was sexy, but it was that night. I will probably never eat salmon nigiri again in my life without thinking about sex."

He laughed.

"You paid for me. I tried to refuse, but you insisted. I kind of knew right then that we were going to blow right by our own rules, but I kept lying to myself for a while longer. Which is why it seemed totally reasonable for me to go back to your house for a drink."

"And . . .?"

"There might have been some kissing."

"Yeah?"

"Yeah. And it was pretty good."

"Just pretty good?"

She knew he was going to kiss her before he did it. Deep, his palm strong on the back of her head, till she was having trouble catching her breath. Then he let her go.

"Couldn't let the other guy get the upper hand?" she teased, because it was either that or fall into his arms and beg him for—for something.

"You just looked so sexy. Talking about it. I could see it all over your face. You get this kind of—dazed look. Your cheeks get pink and your mouth gets soft and your eyes get —sleepy."

He'd caught her between the reverie of memory and the intensity of the present—his hand had moved from the back of her head to her arm, but it still felt like a strong magnet— and she felt that bone-deep craving move down her gut and between her legs.

"But okay, yeah, maybe I didn't want the other guy to be your gold standard."

"The other guy's toast on the kissing front," she said. "He was toast last night. Everything else is just icing. Or butter, I guess."

"Booyah!" he said, and they both laughed. "And then what happened?"

Oh. Right. This part of the story.

No point in sugarcoating it.

"That was when you said it was a mistake and you couldn't do it again—for all the reasons we've talked about. So we called it off for a bit, and for a week or so we avoided each other. Or I avoided you, anyway. I did a couple of pickups and drop-offs from the car, we didn't talk, we didn't email—and then Phoebe got the stomach flu while she was at your house. Actually, both girls. I couldn't take her home because she was violently ill, and you offered for the two of us to stay until Phoebe was more stable. And—"

She tripped and he steadied her, an arm snaking around her waist and drawing her close, so it was harder to walk but she didn't protest because he felt so good. Warm and strong, sturdy and familiar.

"I loved watching you with Clara. I loved that you didn't avoid her like she was plague-stricken. You held her head when she was sick and you sat by her bed and you brought her sips of ginger ale. And—you must have felt the same, because after the girls were both asleep, you came down to the guest room and—"

"We had sex?"

She snuck a peek at him and saw the slight tilt of his smile grow. "You're getting ahead of yourself, dude. First you explained to me why you were so gun-shy."

"Because of Dee."

"You told me that you'd followed your dick—"

He shot her a look and she grinned. "Your words, not mine. And she'd gotten pregnant, and you had to get married. You said you couldn't regret Clara. And given Clara, you knew you'd done the right thing. But—"

"But it wasn't what I would have chosen. I trapped myself."

"Yeah."

He held her gaze for a moment, and she saw the same pain there she'd seen when he'd told her the story that night. Regret, and something else. Something she couldn't quite name.

And just like that other night, he turned away abruptly, closing down her access to what was hurting him.

They walked in silence, the wind brushing damp hair off the back of her neck, making her shiver.

"And then?"

She felt the narrowness of the spit, suddenly, the vastness of space and sea on both sides. "You said you never wanted to make that mistake again. Confusing lust and love. And you said—" She hesitated.

"You said your attraction to me was so intense that you didn't quite trust yourself."

She finished, and he stopped. He looked at the sky, showing her the long line of his throat, already speckled with stubble, the hollow just above the collar of his T-shirt, where a pulse beat.

He pulled his gaze down to meet hers. Held hers prisoner, her blood thrumming everywhere.

"It still is."

The world spun around them.

"I lose my breath when you get close to me," she confessed suddenly. "It's that intense. Like a hand squeezes my lungs. That's never happened to me before."

"Not the first time?" His eyes were bright.

"Not like this. Not this—" She hesitated. What she was trying to describe was the fierceness and suddenness of her arousal. But the words were unfamiliar, and not meant to be said aloud. "Pull," she said feebly, but his eyes lit like he knew exactly what she meant. "Like a whole-body, every-molecule-committed, leaning-toward feeling."

Those eyes. So dark, even in the bright sunshine. So *intent,* so *intense,* so full of emotion.

She wasn't sure he'd looked at her quite that way before. It felt new.

"I know that feeling," he said. "That's how I feel right now."

And she lost her breath, suddenly.

"Trina?"

"Yeah?"

"What was it like when we finally had sex?"

It was killing her. How she was telling him about the past but it was unfolding right this second, too, her breath coming faster, her face hot with it. He was going to be inside her, tonight. And it was going to light her on fire. She was going to burst into flames and burn up, and there would be only a pile of ashes left.

"We barely made it into the guest room. You pushed me back against the door and kissed me. Then you carried me to the bed. And—it was amazing."

He leaned in close.

Whispered.

"But not as amazing as it's going to be tonight."

She was panting. Actually panting, her chest heaving, her breath rasping in her throat.

He brushed his lips across her cheek to her ear and whispered, "Do you want me to kiss you?"

"Yes." She had barely enough breath to make the word audible.

"I will. But not now. When you can't stand it anymore."

18

They ate at Parelli's Pizza, brought the girls home, and got them tucked in.

She took a long, hot shower. Her feet ached, but the rest of her body felt strong and limber from the hike. She'd hurt all over tomorrow, but now she luxuriated in the sensation of the steaming water on her bare skin.

She faced the shower, letting the water tease her nipples to standing, as if the anticipation of what Hunter had taunted her with wasn't enough. She was at least three-quarters of the way to not being able to stand it anymore—the looks he cast her, dirty and full of intention, the surreptitious, light touches, most often in places—like the inside of her wrist—that shouldn't have set her blood boiling but did anyway.

And just—the fun. Life was better with Hunter in it. More alive, more sunlight glancing off water, more whispered secrets, more laughing so hard her stomach ached.

She'd told herself she'd give it today to let things play out before she made a decision about the future. The decision was made—at least in her own mind. She was incapable of turning away from Hunter.

She toweled off and got dressed and went downstairs to the living room.

No Hunter.

She searched the house, but couldn't find him.

What if—

Doubt whispered, raising the hairs on the back of her neck.

What if after all this, after today, what if he still had second thoughts?

He didn't remember everything.

He felt guilty about his marriage.

Something had happened in Afghanistan he didn't understand.

What if she told him she wanted to stay, and he didn't want her to?

She heard footsteps on the back deck, then the sound of the door opening and closing.

"Close your eyes. I have a surprise."

Relief, and pleasure, flooded her. He'd come up behind her and whispered it in her ear, his body just shy of touching hers, his presence rustling her clothes and making hairs stand on end and nerves light up. She felt his breath brush her ear and shivered. Her body bloomed.

She pushed aside her doubts. She pushed aside her fears.

She did as instructed and closed her eyes.

"Come with me."

She followed him, surprisingly disoriented even in a house she had come to think of as her own, out the back kitchen door, down the deck steps. Her senses, in the absence of sight, attuned. To his warm hand wrapped around hers, the charge it conveyed, the scent of fir, cedar, soap, and his skin.

"The old tree house?"

"Mmm-hmm."

He guided her up the steps—a mash-up of true steps and a ladder—his body close behind hers, so close that she found herself swaying toward him as if drawn, trying to feel his hard solidness at her back. He reached around her to open the door for her, and she loved the wrap of that strong arm, the grip and release of muscle against her ribs; she wanted to grab him and turn in his arms and press herself against him to get more of it, full-length.

"Okay. Open."

She opened her eyes. He'd spread a thick quilt on the floor, lit a ring of squat votives in glasses, and set out two slices of cake, an open bottle of red wine, and two glasses.

"Oh." She seemed to have been robbed of more sophisticated speech.

"You like it?"

"Oh, Hunter. I love it. Where did the chocolate cake come from?"

The crinkles at the corners of his eyes deepened. "You know how I 'accidentally' left the leftover pizza box on the table and had to go back in?"

"Oh, clever!"

"That's me."

She searched his face. There was something sad in his eyes. "Hunter. You don't—you don't have to compete with him. With the old you. You know that, right?" She waited for assent, but he was just watching. Listening. "I just want you to know that for me—I'm past that. Past where you need to impress me."

"I know," he said. "But—I don't want to feel like I missed it. Getting to *woo* you. You don't mind?"

"God, *no,* I don't mind at all. I love it. I don't think any woman ever *minds* being wooed."

She sat on the blanket cross-legged and drew one of the plates of cake into her lap. He sat across from her and took the other.

"Do the girls know where we are?" she asked.

"Yup. Told them to text if they need me. But the last time I looked, Clara was mostly asleep and Phoebe's eyes kept fluttering shut. Wine?"

"Yes, sir."

He shot her a sharp look, then poured her a glass, handed it to her, poured his own, and raised it in a toast.

"To the best day I can remember."

Her hand flew to her throat. "Oh."

He tilted his head, a question in his eyes.

"It's the best day I remember, too." She lifted her glass again and touched it lightly to his. The chime of glass on glass shimmered up her arm. "To outdoing yourself." She smiled mischievously at him. "Last time, we ate the chocolate cake at Parelli's with the girls."

"*Damn.* I thought at least the cake was a new touch."

"I'm teasing you," she admitted. "There was no chocolate cake last time."

He laughed. "Guess I'm kind of an easy mark, huh?"

"Yeah, just think how bad I could mess with your head if I wanted to."

She sipped her wine. She didn't know crap about wine,

except that there were some that went down so easy she knew they had to be expensive. This was one of those. It soothed her mouth and throat, slid down and warmed her all over. She didn't drink often, had drunk almost never when Hunter was deployed and she'd been in charge of Phoebe and Clara, only girls' nights here and there with good friends. So she was a lightweight. And in a few sips she could feel the slight hum under her lips and in her feet that preceded the loss of inhibition. Not that she needed any less. Seven-eighths, she thought. Seven-eighths of the way to blazing with impatience. Seven-eighths of the way to crawling across the floor and taking his mouth for her own.

"Oh. Wow. This is good." She pulled a bite of cake, moist, rich, and flavorful, slowly off her fork, savoring, and caught him watching her mouth.

Nine-tenths.

"Do that again," he said, eyes dark.

Eleven-twelfths. She did it again, her eyes on his this time. Licked the remaining dark chocolate icing off the fork when she was done, and then, purely for the effect she knew it would have on him, tipped her gaze down to the fly of his khaki shorts, where there was definite action.

"Trina."

She'd turned his voice rough, into almost a plea. But there was nothing she could do to him that she couldn't feel, too, no way to give him pleasure without it touching her. Her nipples were tight knots, her skin tuned, receptive. She had turned to something molten, and she wanted to pour her liquid self all over him, into him.

She set her plate on the floor, her fork beside her mostly uneaten cake. Crawled across the floor to him. He stretched his legs out and leaned on his hands, and she climbed over him and straddled him.

She settled herself so she could feel his erection pressing up against the seam of her jeans.

"Hunter."

"Mmm-hmm."

He was teasing her, pretending nonchalance, but there was no doubt in her head she was messing with him. Even if she hadn't been able to feel him shifting restlessly against her through layers of clothing, his eyes wouldn't leave hers and they were so dark now they were almost black, and there was a flush under his tanned skin.

"I can't stand it any—"

But she didn't get to finish. His mouth cut off the last word.

19

He wanted more of what he'd already had, more of the softness of her lips, the plumpness of that bottom one and the way she squeaked and whimpered when he licked it, then bit it. More of her taste, familiar and delicious, something elemental and personal under the wine and chocolate. More of the way her skin smelled, this close, nothing he could put words to, but so essentially *her* that it made him grabby, his fingers rucked into her hair, into her clothes, ready to clutch and tear and *take*. More of her tongue, the slide of it against his own, the way she challenged him for control of the kiss. He grabbed the back of her head and asserted himself, and he heard her moan, felt her soften. *Fuck yes. More.*

But he wanted other things, too. What he didn't have yet, the soft, hot, slick center of her. Her skin bare and satiny, the yielding curves and the strength underneath.

He'd never wanted anyone this much—except he *had*. *Before.*

And he was aware that unlike him, she held all of their

history in her head and her heart, and this must be fucking weird for her. So he took care with her. Went slow. Tried to think about how this was the same and different for her. To feel around in his own lost memory, groping for purchase, to see if he could follow instinct to make it old and new, familiar and mind-blowing.

That was what he wanted to do for her. He wanted to give her exactly what she craved in a way she'd never imagined before.

So he kissed her every way he could think of. Soft and slow and sweet, nibbling and stroking, drawing her out to meet him. And then so hard it was like fucking, his tongue aggressive, almost mean, on the tenderest parts of her mouth.

She liked it. She liked it all. He could feel her open up and spread out, like something unfurling in sunlight. Her body giving itself up to him.

He was so hard it hurt, his cock sandwiched between his own body and hers, restricted by too many layers of clothes, straining at its own skin. She was rocking now, her hips tipping and tilting, the pressure increasing as she went after what she needed, and all the while the kisses got hotter and wetter and wilder, her moans longer and less restrained.

He wanted to know, though. He had to know.

"Is it like you remember?"

"Stop. It doesn't matter." She was breathless. Her mouth so red it was hard for him not to dive back in, kiss it again.

"It matters to me."

"Why?"

"Because I don't remember. And I wish I did."

"I do remember. And I wish I didn't."

"Why?"

"Because I want to be here. Just here. Don't you? Not *before* or in the future or anything. In this very moment. Kiss me again."

So he did. *I want to be here. Kiss me again.* He could do that.

He slid a hand under her shirt, felt the smooth, hot skin of her belly, spread his fingers wide to touch as much of her at once as he could. His thumb brushed the waistband of her jeans, his pinky the lace of her bra, and it suddenly seemed imperative that he be able to see her, touch her, taste more, all, of her.

He peeled her T-shirt over her head and leaned back to see, which pushed him tighter against the seam of her jeans. He growled at the feel of that and the sight of her, soft and abundant, cupped in lace, her nipples dark points he could see through the weave of the thread.

He unhooked her bra, and she stretched luxuriously and arched her back to push herself toward his face, and suddenly he found himself with her more-than-a-handful breasts, one in each hand, not sure what the hell to do with so much awesomeness at once other than to bury his face.

"I don't want to hurt you." He wasn't clean shaven, not this late in the day.

"It feels good."

She was red where he'd rubbed and he really fucking liked that—marking her that way. He liked anything and everything she liked.

And now, suddenly, moved by generosity edged hard with greed, he had to make her squirm, had to make her whimper and moan and flail and rub against him. He wanted desperately to make her feel good because it made him feel *so fucking good.*

The instant his lips closed on her nipple, she gave him exactly what he was looking for. A low, dark moan in the back of her throat. The plummet of her hips against his straining cock. And the thrust of her breast, all soft, warm, Trina-scented bare skin, into his mouth—her voice breaking on "More, Hunter, please."

He worked that nipple with his lips, his tongue, easing her up from flicks to light suckling to full pulls, feeling how her hips changed to match him, how her moans and words rose and tightened. The motion of her body against his had found a steadier rhythm now, a mounting pressure and tension, as she guided them both toward her goal.

"Hunter?"

"Mmm-hmm?"

He didn't let her nipple go. He had the other one in his fingers, now, flicking, pinching, twisting, trying to figure out exactly what drove her crazy, lingering when she made that tight lost sound in her chest, when she rocked harder against him.

"I want you—inside me."

It was his turn to moan. He freed both her nipples and she made a small sound of protest, but then he yanked his T-shirt over his head and she spread both her hands over his chest and the feeling was so unexpectedly amazing, the warmth of her palms all over his skin, her thumbs teasing his nipples like he'd teased hers a moment earlier, and then her hands were on the button of his jeans, the zipper—

She hesitated a moment, then said, "Holy fuck, Hunter, you're so big."

He bucked against the shockingly cool touch of the palm of her hand, and a deep moan broke from his lips.

She surprised him by laughing.

"What?"

"I didn't want to deprive you. Of hearing it again."

"Oh, God. *Right.*" She'd done this all before, and remembered well.

"Mmm-hmm. So fucking hot. The way you act like I'm the hottest thing ever."

"Not acting," he corrected. "You *are* the hottest thing ever. You blow my mind."

She eased his jeans and briefs down enough that she could grasp him in her fist, then dipped her head to take him in her mouth. Clutched him tight in the heat and wet, her lips rounding him, stretched and red, her shiny blond hair shimmering in the flickering light as she moved up and down in his lap, as if she knew *exactly* what she was doing, as if—

As if she'd done it tens of times before.

Right.

"You're—so—good—at—that—"

She paused, her breath hot and silky against the wetness she'd left on his throbbing cock. "I love giving you head. Always have."

She ran her tongue across the super-sensitive base of the head and he couldn't help himself, he thrust. Instead of drawing back, she moved farther down on him so he was buried almost to the hilt.

It jacked him up so fast that for a split second he was sure he was going to come in her mouth. Then, with a super-human effort, he reasserted control over himself and gently drew her up.

"You said you wanted me inside you. Did you mean it?"

"Fuck yeah."

He loved that word on her lips. "Take your shorts off."

He shed his jeans and briefs while she slid out of her shorts. She wore only a black lace thong. She lay back, thighs together, and there was something so hot about that juxtaposition, the plump ivory of thighs and the black vee of lace.

"Look at you. All demure."

"God, no. Just so turned on I can't help rubbing my thighs together."

He saw the subtle press of muscle now as she crossed and squeezed. "Fuck."

"That's the idea."

He wanted to tease her open and lick the wet, sloppy center of her. Or pry her open. That would work, too. Whatever it took to get to the black lace truth of her.

"Should I take them off?"

"Leave them on. God. I can't decide. If I want you to spread your legs for me or if I want to make you want to spread them or if I want to make you spread them whether you want to or not."

She made an incoherent sound.

"Sorry? Didn't understand you. Could you say that again more clearly?"

"Hunter."

He knelt over her and licked the seam of her thighs where they met, from knee to vee. When his tongue touched black lace she cried out and he withdrew his touch. He did it again, her thighs slowly drifting apart so his tongue found the space between them. This time when he licked her through her panties and she whimpered, he didn't stop. With one finger he drew them aside. Wet. Ruined. And he ruined them worse with his tongue, with his whole face buried against her. God, she was sweet.

"Hunter!"

He lifted his face and smirked at her. "Is that 'yes, Hunter, please'? Or 'no, Hunter, please, stop'?"

"Oh. Ohhhhh—"

That was the sound of the tip of his tongue finding her clit. Slipping back and forth over it while she arched up to try to get more contact.

The way he'd pictured her in bed, after that first night she'd climbed in with him? Apparently, that had been memory, not fantasy. But now it felt like fantasy come true.

He gave her his finger, deep inside her.

"You want more?"

Her response wasn't quite an actual word.

He drew back, knelt beside her. Reached for a condom and rolled it down.

She grabbed him. Squeezed, ran a thumb up the length along the ridge, over the head, that *look* in her eyes. Like she liked what she saw and felt, a lot.

He braced himself over her. Before his cock even made contact with her, he could feel her heat, and every muscle in his body strained toward it, the injured ones griping but not enough to stop him. And then he was in her, just an inch, pressing toward what he desperately wanted—the softness and heat of her, the sense of being surrounded, the pleasure of her tightness. He craved connection with her. He wanted to destroy all the distance his forgetfulness had created.

She moaned as he buried himself. Each stroke brought another moan, his body trying harder to turn itself inside out inside her, her hips lifting, his pressing her down, her breath speeding, her eyes closing.

Then with a cry she was clenching around him, coming hard, her body twisting—but it was her voice, her words, cracked and wispy, that took him over: "I missed you, Hunter."

He gave himself up, poured himself out, released what he'd lost and what he'd tried to hold onto, fell into what was left of what he hadn't known was his.

"Oh, *God,* Trina, I missed you, too."

And even though they both knew it was a lie, it was the whole perfect fucking truth.

20

H e was the first one to hear the crying. At first he thought it was a child, and he ran toward the sound.

A woman. Behind a wall of rubble, but if he peeked through, he could just see her, crouched there, babbling in Pashto. Her eyes panicked in the dark.

Her pleas . . .

Her eyes . . .

He never let himself think about the way Dee had died. The violent, dirty surprise of it. The pain, the dust, the debris. She would have been buried. If the explosion hadn't killed her, she would have been crushed or suffocated.

She might have known she was dying.

She would have looked just like this woman.

Suddenly he was digging, clawing, as if he were trying to claw at the thing that had him around the throat, around the chest, as if he were trying to rip away the thing that had stolen his breath.

He had to get her out.

He might have been calling her name.

And in the darkness he saw her, her face, her eyes—

And when the second explosion came, he had time to see the expression on her face, shocked and accusing.

Dee's face.

The world slid away.

He was awake in the dark. For a long moment, he couldn't remember, drowning in panic. Where he was. Why he was there.

There was a body beside his.

A woman's body.

His heart jangled against the cage of his ribs.

Not a body. A living woman.

Not Dee.

Trina.

The clock glowing on Trina's bedside table said it was five a.m.

He'd walked her back from the tree house last night, late, both of them stumbling and giddy. He'd tucked her into bed in the guest room, then lain down beside her, just for a second. But then she'd rolled close and kissed him and he'd had no way to resist her pull. He was armorless.

The dream felt real, and what had happened last night in the tree house felt like a dream.

"You okay?" she whispered, in the dark.

"No," he said.

She rolled toward him, wrapping her warmth around him. But where last night it had felt like such a gift, her body giving to his, this morning it felt like a threat. He couldn't help it; he flinched.

He felt her equal and opposite reaction, the way she withdrew and stiffened, and he wanted to take it back, but he couldn't.

"Hunter, what is it?"

"I remembered. I saw her. She was buried in there, and she couldn't get out, and I was trying to save her."

"To save the woman who was buried under rubble?"

"To save Dee."

She made a small, shocked noise.

"It was Dee. I saw her in there, and—I'd never thought about it before. How she died. I'd made myself never think about it. And I couldn't save her. It was Dee."

"In the dream?"

"No. Not a dream. A memory."

"You couldn't have remembered her there, Hunter. She wasn't there."

His chest hurt. Where he'd been split open, but every-where else, too. A squeezing, twisting sensation. "She was there, the day I was injured. In my head. It was her, and I couldn't save her."

"Hunter," she repeated, "It wasn't Dee. It was some other woman. It wasn't Dee you couldn't—"

"I know!"

His voice was sharp in the dark. It was the first time he'd ever raised his voice to her, and he felt her flinch.

He took a deep breath. "Dee did this thing. She—she'd change herself. For me. Like she cut her hair and put high-lights in it, and she said, 'I know you like Tanya Freeny's hair.' I'd once said that, but only because she said, 'What do you think of Tanya Freeny's hair?' and I said, 'I like it.' She lost weight, even though she wasn't really heavy. Just—solid. And then she said, 'I know skinny's more your type.' I never said that. I know I never said that. I'd never say something like that. It's not even true."

He'd never told this to anyone. He could tell he'd never told Trina before, not only because of the surprise and pain on her face, but because of how the words felt coming out of him. Squeezed and narrow. But even though it hurt to say it, he couldn't stop.

"One time she took cooking classes. She said, 'I know you wish I were a better cook.' Even though I swear, I never said anything like that to her. I tried never to say the things in my head, the doubts—but she heard them anyway, somehow. She didn't say, 'I thought if I did this, you might fall in love with me,' but it was so clear. It was like she was shouting it all the time. Every time she baked me cookies or came home with a six-pack of my favorite beer or—there were things she didn't like to do in bed, and I said she shouldn't, she didn't have to, but she did, because—"

His voice broke, remembering. All the times she'd come home with a new look or newly gained knowledge or a gift. The way she'd gagged, trying to take him deeper, trying so hard to be the woman she was sure he wanted.

The futility of it.

"She was trying to make me love her. I couldn't love her, Trina. I tried. And tried. And then—

"We had a fight, right before she deployed. Where she said, 'Just tell me, Hunter. Tell me what I can do to make this marriage work.' And I knew. I knew I had to tell her the truth. Not right then, because she was leaving, but I had to tell her I wanted a divorce. Because it was so damn unfair to her, what I'd done to her. I had to give her another chance. To find someone who would love her the way she deserved."

Trina was very still, very quiet. "But she didn't come home."

He shook his head. "No. She didn't come home."

"It wasn't your fault, Hunter. You did the very best you could."

"It was," he said. "It *was* my fault because I knew, even that first time I had sex with her, that I couldn't do what she wanted me to do. But I wanted her, so I lied to myself. I told myself that I could do it, that it would just take time, that I would fall in love with her. As if all it would take was an effort of will. No one is going to—"

His voice broke, but he pressed on, because he had to, because it was penance. It was only what he deserved. "No one will ever love her the way she deserved to be loved now. I took that away from her. Maybe I didn't kill her, but because I was selfish, she will never have that life."

"Hunter. Those things weren't in your control. That woman's death. Dee's death. How much you love some—"

"Don't try to fix it, Trina. Okay? Don't fucking try to fix it."

It was so quiet in the room that he could hear the wind blowing through the trees outside.

"Do you want me to make you stop thinking about it?"

He did. Desperately. He'd remembered and forgotten all the wrong things, and he knew she could make it better, if only for a little while. But—

She slid down the length of his body, and he felt his resolve slipping. She rucked his T-shirt up and her breath swept the flat of his abs, above the waistband of his boxers. Her fingers were much surer now than they'd been earlier. "Lift up," she instructed.

He hesitated.

"I don't know what's in my own head. I shouldn't."

"Then don't listen to your head right now. Lift up."

He did, and she slid his boxers down, and came back to nuzzle his cock, growing heavy now, reaching for her. She opened her mouth and let him in, but this time she kept him there only long enough to make him slick and hard, then released him and rose up over him.

She reached for the box of condoms on the nightstand, rolled one on him, and eased herself down on him, her body parting to admit him, and then lowered herself in an abrupt plunge that made his stomach sink and swirl like a roller-coaster plummet.

And it was so good, so sweet and dark and hot and wet, and she leaned down and matched her mouth to his, so they could feel each other that way, too, vulnerable parts to vulnerable parts, the intimacy so fierce and raw.

Then she eased back, taking him deep and—rather than rising and plunging—rubbing herself tight over his pubic bone. He saw the look in her eyes, that searching-for-something-just-out-of-reach expression.

"What do you need?"

She cupped her breast and he took the tight nipple in his mouth, his fingers stroking the other one, and she made a hoarse sound and her movements got more ferocious. She rode him like that, her breasts in his mouth and his hand, his other hand curved from her hip around her ass, an ache blooming hard up his spine until he came just a second ahead of her, his last fierce push to inhabit her fully pressing her over the edge until he had to stifle her cries with his mouth.

21

He was gone when she woke up. She lay there and stared at the sun chinking through the blinds and she ached all over from her exertions yesterday, and that deep pain felt like a messenger of bad news.

He could be downstairs making her breakfast. He could be preparing a tray to bring up to her. He would show up in the doorway and say, "Look what I made for you!" and he would set it across her lap. Thank her for being there for him when he'd been hurting in the middle of the night. Apologize for having yelled at her. Tell her she'd done it, she'd fixed it, just like she'd said she would.

Only she knew he wasn't, and he wouldn't.

After a while, she got out of bed and took a long, hot shower. She dressed in jeans and a dark gray fitted T-shirt, and she went out into the kitchen and made herself a bowl of granola. She checked on the girls, who were rollerblading in the street outside the house.

She crossed into the backyard, walked through the woods on what had become almost a well-trodden path, and found him just where she'd known he'd be. Up the tree. He'd just drilled a hole inside a larger hole.

"What are you doing?"

"Getting ready to sink a TAB," he said.

She wanted to see it. She wanted to watch as the tree house took shape, as he anchored it, as he built it. She wanted to design it and make it hers. Theirs.

She wanted to stay.

Part of her had probably always known she didn't want to go. Part of her had always known that L.A. was a poor consolation prize for what she and Phoebe couldn't have.

"Tomorrow's Saturday."

It was disconcerting, talking up at him, but she knew she had no choice. She knew he wouldn't, couldn't, face her right now.

He touched the edge of the hole he'd drilled, testing. Not looking down at her. But she knew that he knew she was there. His whole body radiated awareness and tension.

She could walk away, but she'd never forgive herself. If she didn't lay everything on the line, despite the fact that she knew it wouldn't change the way he felt. Or didn't feel.

"I don't have to go, Hunter. I could call Stefan and tell him to offer the job to someone else. I could say I changed my mind. That I—"

She was going to lose her nerve if she didn't just spit it out.

"—That I love you. And I don't need any other reason to stay."

She took a deep breath.

He'd stopped moving. He rested in his harness, his body an L, his legs slightly bent against the tree trunk. And then slowly he lowered himself, walking down the solid column of the tree's strength, until his feet were on the ground again. His eyes drilled into her.

"You think you don't." His voice was low. Angry. "You think you don't, now, but you will. I know you want me to ask you to stay. But if I do that, a week, a month, a year from now, you'll be looking at me with big Bambi eyes, asking what you can do to make things okay."

She shook her head, tears filling her eyes. "That's not true, Hunter."

"You'll end up hating me for not giving you what you need."

"No. No."

"And I'll hate you for wanting more than I can give."

It was surprising how much that hurt. Like something splintering in her chest. The last few days, the blooming tenderness between them, the joy, the ferocious need—that he could have been with her through all of that and still *doubt.*

She got angry, then. Fast, like the anger had been waiting right beneath the surface, boiling there, brewing under her patience with the two-steps-forward-and-one-back, the forbidden connections in the dark, the slow dance in the light.

"Don't fucking tell me that, Hunter. Don't tell me you *can't* do it. Don't tell me what you can and can't give. I've seen you. I know you. And you fell in love with me. So if you're not feeling it now, it's not because you can't."

She took a deep breath.

"It's because you *won't.*"

She was breathless and furious.

"You loved me, Hunter. I know you did."

He turned away, gazed up for a moment at the thick TABs protruding from the tree. Like strange robotic branches grafted on, half organic, half man-made.

"Maybe I did."

When he looked at her again, it was almost blankly, absently, the way he'd looked at her those first couple of days, as if she were vaguely familiar but he couldn't quite place her.

"But I won't let you give up your life waiting for it to happen again."

There was such an awful finality in his voice. She felt like the wind had been knocked out of her.

But the sound, the one like air going out of someone who'd been punched in the stomach, wasn't her.

They both turned.

Clara was standing at the edge of the clearing. Stock still, eyes wide.

Hunter started toward her. "Clara!"

But she was already running away.

22

Trina found Clara up in the old tree house, facedown on the bed.

She sat beside her almost-daughter and stroked her hair, until Clara said in a soft, tear-choked voice, "If he loved you, would you stay?"

Oh, *God.*

For a moment, it felt so complicated. The job, the possibility of Phoebe getting to know her biological father . . .

Hunter.

Clara.

It seemed important, no matter how much it might hurt both of them, for her to tell the truth, so she took a deep breath and said, "Yes. But he doesn't. He can't, right now."

"You said he *won't.* You said he's choosing not to."

She had. And she believed it. But she also knew it was more complex than that.

"Sometimes—sometimes for grown-ups, things don't feel exactly like choices. It's like everything that's happened to you before adds up to something—inevitable."

"I hate him," Clara said. "I hate him for making you leave."

Trina's throat felt so tight she could barely speak, and all that mattered to her in that moment was trying to make this okay for Clara. And for Hunter. So the two of them could begin the process of rebuilding their family.

It hurt, so much, but it was what needed to happen now.

"He's not making me leave. I know what you heard, and what it must have sounded like, but grown-ups are complicated. Even though it sounded like a fight, we both know I need to leave. He can't just magically love me. Love isn't like a switch you can turn on and off."

Though God knew, she wished it were. So she could stop wanting what she couldn't have. She'd worked so hard to forget Stefan, to get away from the experience of wishing for what wouldn't happen, only to find herself right back where she'd started.

"I wish he'd never gotten amnesia," Clara said.

Her voice had softened a little, some of the tension easing from her skinny little body, and Trina took her first full breath in what felt like hours. "Me too," she said. "But maybe it wouldn't have worked out anyway. He was gone a long time. People change a lot in a year. They see things and do things that change what they want out of life. You know—" she told Clara. "You know this has *nothing* to do with you, right? You know I—"

There was no way she was getting through this without tears, so she gave up right then. "You know I love you so much. You know I don't want to leave you. You know I would stay if I felt like I could. You know I will always be available if you need me. You can call, you can email, and if you really need me, you can ask me, and I'll come."

"If something bad happened, and I needed, like, a substitute mom, you'd come?"

"Absolutely."

Clara sat up and threw her arms around Trina and the two of them sat there, legs bunched under them on the bed, clinging to each other and crying, until neither of them had any tears left.

"I won't tell Phoebe," Clara said suddenly.

"You won't tell her what?"

"What I heard you and Daddy say. She'd be sad, too. We both thought—we both thought you were changing your mind. That things were going back to the way they used to be."

"Oh," Trina said, suddenly getting it. That she and Hunter hadn't been fooling anyone, *before*. That the girls had known full well just how serious their parents had been. That they'd built their own castle of expectations, their own fantasies for the future. And they'd had them built up and torn down more than once, just as she had.

Why hadn't she seen that?

Because she'd been too busy riding her own roller coaster.

"We weren't careful," she said. "We weren't as careful as we should have been. We should have been more discreet."

But part of her suspected that they'd simply underestimated the intuitive powers of two twelve-year-old girls.

Part of her wanted to ask Clara not to tell Phoebe what she'd overheard. Not to spread the pain any farther. But the other part of her knew that wouldn't be fair. That Clara needed to be able to talk about what had happened, to share her suffering with the only other person who might have a chance of understanding it.

"You can tell her, sweetheart. And I'll talk to her, too, okay? So she knows—it's all going to be okay."

Although she wasn't sure exactly how she would convince Phoebe of that fact, when she hardly believed it herself.

23

"I know you're angry."

That was the understatement of the year.

"Phoebe, please."

But you couldn't make a stubborn twelve-year-old talk.

They'd left early in the morning for the airport, even though their flight to L.A. wasn't scheduled to leave till late afternoon. She just couldn't take any more of Hunter's attempts at normalcy.

So just after breakfast, she'd let the shuttle driver hoist their suitcases on board, then slid in beside Phoebe. They were the only two passengers and they'd sat in the way back, so they had a little privacy. Not that it mattered, because an angry twelve-year-old girl was like a black hole, sucking all conversation and emotion in.

"I tried, Phoebe."

Trina supposed she was overdue. She'd read the books; she knew the children of split households often went through long periods of blaming the remaining parent for the absence of the distant one. She'd been lucky, and Phoebe had never gotten angry at her in that way. She hadn't really gotten angry at Stefan, either. She'd just . . . accepted the situation. So maybe it was time for a little anger.

Trina certainly was angry. Angry at Hunter, because it was easier, and cleaner, than feeling anything else. She would not —*could* not—feel anything else. But she could be angry at him for shutting her out. Last night—she'd cooked the chili she'd promised Clara, and cornbread, and brownies—he'd treated both her and Phoebe the way he had when they'd first met. As if they were valued guests—the relatives of an important co-worker or friend, perhaps.

She had always known that in hoping for him to love her again, she'd been on the most tenuous, uncertain ground. Since the promise he'd made before his deployment, he'd never again asked her to have faith in him, to believe that things would turn out well, or to risk her heart for him. She'd given him all her love and trust because it had been the only thing she knew how to do. Because the alternative—to give up on him—had felt unthinkable.

So she didn't blame him for *her* pain.

But she *was* furious with him for hurting Phoebe and Clara.

Phoebe and Clara's matching sad, gray faces had broken Trina's heart. Maybe her heart was already most of the way broken, but there had been little fragments still held together. The girls' grief had shattered what was left.

But most of all, Trina was angry at herself. Because she'd foreseen this all, and she'd still allowed herself the destructive fantasy that somehow it would work out. She'd let herself believe that the joy she'd felt with Hunter, the joy she'd felt with the girls in the months that Hunter had been gone, was something permanent that belonged to her. When she knew, perfectly well, men left. *Family* was her and Phoebe.

The definition of insanity is doing the same thing twice and expecting different results.

He'd given her a preview of this grief the day he'd come home, and *still* she'd let herself be drawn back into the heat and temptation of him. Like a seventeen-year-old girl whose hormones were in control.

Like Hunter, who had followed his dick into the thorny tangle of his marriage with Dee.

She touched Phoebe's shoulder. "I'm so, so sorry, baby."

Finally, her daughter turned to look at her, her face streaked with tears. Phoebe's eyes searched hers, looking for . . . Trina wasn't sure. But whatever she saw, Phoebe's face softened, the anger slipping away. "It's not your fault, Mom."

It was that, more than anything, that finally loosed Trina's tears, and the two of them cried in the backseat of that grimy shuttle, arms around each other, mourning what was lost and grateful for what they still had.

After that, they talked about L.A. About how it was different from what Phoebe had known before, how the height and bustle of it, and even the palm-tree-sunniness of it, would feel foreign at first, but that eventually it would feel more comfortable, like a worn-in sweatshirt.

The first of the airport signs came into view, and Trina touched Phoebe's shoulder and pointed. The official beginning of the journey.

Or that's what it was supposed to be.

Departures.

And that, right there, was the truth of it. It should feel like a new beginning, but even with Phoebe's hand tucked snugly into hers, squeezing reassuringly, it felt like the end.

24

He'd hugged them goodbye at the curb.

He'd kept it as brief and distant as possible, trying not to catch the layers of Trina's scent—floral shampoo, sharp Ivory soap, lavender deodorant, the smell of her skin, her secret sweet-salty center. Releasing her before the press of her body could penetrate his numbness.

Trying not to crave the bear hugs he'd gotten into the habit of with Phoebe at some point in the last week, but just giving her a kindly uncle's careful squeeze.

She was not his daughter. She was Stefan Spencer's daughter, and if Stefan Spencer had never done anything particularly heroic, neither had he pretended to have more to give than he did.

He knew it was wrong, putting them in a shuttle and sending them away, but he hadn't been able to stand the thought of riding in the car with them.

His head hurt.

He kept seeing Dee's eyes over and over again, reminding him of what he'd taken away from her.

Trina's eyes held some of that, too. The accusation.

She hadn't asked him to drive them to the airport, and he hadn't offered.

Like last night. She hadn't come to his room, and when the dark hours stretched without her, he hadn't gone to her, either. It wasn't pride. It was what was best for her.

The shuttle pulled away from the curb in front of his house and he was left with Clara, who was sobbing.

He put his arms around her because that was what he knew he should do, but it was like he was touching her through layers of thick cotton wool. Her grief couldn't reach him, so all he could do was pat her and murmur things that were true but not felt.

Clara was murmuring something indistinct into his shirt, over and over. He tilted his head to listen.

"You should have made them stay."

But it wasn't true. It wasn't that he should have made them stay. It was that he never should have led them on in the first place. He was angry at himself—or rather, he was angry at that other guy, that pre-deployment Hunter—for making them—Trina, Phoebe, *and* Clara—believe in happily-ever-after.

"They don't belong here, baby. They were just staying here while I was gone, but now that I'm back, they have to get on with their lives. Trina has a special job that's perfect for her. Phoebe needs to know her father."

"*You're* her father."

His heart gave a funny, misguided hiccup of hope, as if somehow Clara's saying it might make it true, but then he thought of the look on Trina's face after he'd said he didn't want her to wait around for him to love her again. Closed.

Finished. And that was what he'd wanted. To get her to see that hanging around hoping for him to give her what she wanted would end badly, sooner or later. Better sooner than later.

"No, baby, I'm not her father. She has a father. Stefan Spencer."

Clara's face turned pink and her eyes got big.

She'd always gotten angry exactly that way, ever since she was a baby.

"Then you're not *my* father, either."

She punctuated her words with a stamp of her foot and stormed into the house.

He knew he should go after her. He should set her straight. He should say, *I am your father, and I love you so much.*

But maybe he hadn't loved her enough. He had left her so many times. Duty first, he'd thought. But maybe that was all wrong. Maybe that was his biggest mistake.

He didn't know how long he stood there in front of the house, not moving. His heart pounding, breath coming so hard he could hear it rasping in his throat. Darkness sinking over him, over the room in the building thousands of miles away, the impenetrable black behind the ragged concrete, and then those *eyes*. Grief and guilt bound tight around his chest.

When he came back to himself and went inside, Clara's room had been ransacked, and Clara herself was nowhere to be found.

He searched the house from top to bottom, as carefully as he could, holding panic at arm's length. He searched first in the hiding places she'd favored as a little girl, but when that didn't pan out, he opened cabinets and crawl spaces, then planted himself facedown on the floor to peer under beds where dust hadn't been disturbed for years. In the master bedroom closet, he thrust his hand through the small collection of Dee's clothes he had saved for Clara and swept it across the shelf behind, even though logic told him she couldn't possibly be hiding there.

His grasping fingertips brushed an object, and something clicked in his mind. Not memory. Recognition. He knew the shape, size, and feel of it.

His mind rejected the possibility even as he clutched it, drew it out of the tangle of musty clothes, and shoved it into his jeans pocket as if he were pushing it back down through layers of memory.

There wasn't time to think about what it might mean. There was only Clara and figuring out where she'd gone.

Leaving the empty house behind, he raced into the yard. Climbed into Clara's tree house. No sign of her. Climbed down again. Harnessed himself to the new tree. It occurred to him, clipping in at intervals to peer through the branches, that he no longer cared about building the tree house. That from almost the beginning he had been building it for Trina, to see what she would put inside it, to see how she would stamp it as hers. To feel like they were building something together, their creations intertwined until afterward you could hardly say what was her and what was him.

The thought choked him, and he thought maybe he'd scrap the project, tear out the TABs and brackets and frame he'd built. It would take as long to dismantle it as it had taken to build it, but it would be something to do, something to occupy himself with.

He tromped around the woods, looking for her. Came

back and threw open the door of the toolshed, though he knew as he did that it was a futile gesture. Clara hadn't set foot in that toolshed in years, terrified of its dark corners. He didn't bother making a study of the little room, where—she had correctly observed—there were spiders aplenty, and snakes, too.

No, she was gone.

And the thing he was most ashamed of was that he was jealous of her, as he was jealous of Trina and Phoebe, because all of them could run away from him and what was inside his head.

"Hunter?"

The three men had materialized on their bicycles like some kind of low-key Hells Angels. Nate dismounted first and reached him.

"What are you doing here?"

"We're on our way back. From the trip." Nate shot a look at the contents of his overloaded bike. The three men were scruffily bearded and definitely the worse for wear.

"Thought we'd maybe snag some yard space and a shower if you guys were feeling generous."

What did *generous* have to do with *numb*?

He couldn't figure it out. It was like a math problem his brain was too tired to solve. He opened his mouth to say something, then closed it. When he finally spoke, the words that came out had nothing to do with Nate's question.

"I can't find Clara."

25

While Nate, Griff, and Jake combed the neighborhood in a grid system they'd laid out, Hunter started in on a more systematic search of the house and yard. Jake had instructed him not to reject any possible hiding spot, no matter how implausible. "Kids can make themselves a lot smaller than you think."

They were here, all of them, helping him. They'd shown up, really more like guardian angels than Hells Angels. No blame, no questions, just arms slung here and there across his shoulders, and Jake, a guy he barely knew, giving him that steady-eyed reassuring look, like *Dude, I know you're freaking out and I would be, too, but it's gonna be okay.*

It just felt so far from okay.

He finished the house and started in on the woods again, combing as thoroughly as he could, trying to see the maze of it as a grid like the one they'd laid out over the neighborhood. He peeked into every corner of the tree house, under the daybed, in all the cabinets, even the ones he knew were too small to hide a preteen girl.

He came out of the woods into the sunlight of the back-yard and stood there, letting the sun's brilliance blaze into his eyes, as if it might illuminate his next move.

He was listening with half his self for a call from inside, or the sound of Jake or Nate or Griff hailing him from the neighborhood, or, best of all, the music of Clara's voice sifting through the ordinary forest sounds. But all he heard was trees moving in the breeze and the tree house creaking just slightly on its perch. The distant highway and a lawn being mowed. Children playing, but not his child.

If something had happened to her, he would never forgive himself. Trina, who loved Clara with a mother's love, would never forgive him.

Except he knew that wasn't true. Trina had held him blameless for the woman in the darkness. For Dee's death.

That blanched, shocked face, the accusation—

With a tremendous effort he pulled himself back from that black hole.

Those things weren't in your control. That woman's death. Dee's death. How much you love some—

She'd been about to tell him, *You can't control how much you love someone,* when he'd cut her off. Furious. He'd been furious.

He wanted—

He wanted to believe her.

His chest ached, something rising and looming just behind the veil of numbness.

He couldn't.

He pushed it down again and the veil held.

Find Clara.

There was just the toolshed left.

He blinked against the power of the sun and strode toward the shack. Threw the door open. In that transition from absolute blinding sun to pure black, the world vanished and he could see less than nothing, so the first thing he knew was the sniffles, the small, helpless sounds in the dark, and then, like something rising to the surface of memory, a face in the dark, pale, frightened. Eyes. For a moment he grappled with it and crossed over between worlds, the impulse to tear at the concrete between them almost overwhelming, his fingernails burning, dust rasping his lungs, because she needed his help and he would have done anything, *anything,* to protect her.

"Daddy!" said the white face with the big eyes, and it was, suddenly, Clara.

Clara, crying, her arms thrown around him.

"God, Clara! You scared me so bad."

"I'm sorry, Daddy! I'm sorry! I'm sorry!"

The words were all murky wet with tears, and she was sobbing against his chest.

And the numbness parted like a curtain and he felt the weight of the guilt he'd carried, the spiky outlines of fear that had lurked in all the dark corners of his mind, and he was—

He was crying, too. For the woman in the dream, in the wrecked building. For himself, lost in his own mind, and for Trina, for what she'd lost. For all of them. Because there were just so many damn ways it was possible to be in the dark, alone.

But most of all, for Dee, because he never had. Because he'd buried her deeper than lost memory, rather than feel what he was feeling now.

He clung to Clara and her sobs drowned out the quiet

sounds of his grief and his tears got lost amidst hers, and he comforted them both by stroking her hair and whispering "shhhh" into her ear, the way he had when she was a colicky infant.

It worked. On her, and on him. The grief, unleashed, dissipated. Felt manageable again. And she subsided to hiccups and sighs against him. Between the tortured little breaths, she informed him:

"Phoebe and I thought if I were missing you'd have to call Trina to help look for me and then they wouldn't go, and if they didn't go then Trina's job would be gone and they would have come back for good."

He heard the sharp intake of breath behind him, but he didn't lift his head from his daughter's hair, fragrant and soft.

"That was—foolish. And *brave*."

"She's the best," Clara said on a sob. "She makes everything fun."

Hunter squeezed his daughter tighter, and he thought of Lakeshore and the raft, the sparkle of sun on water and mischief in Trina's eyes, the torment of her body slipping past his as they kidded and teased. Thought of the spit and how it felt to walk out on the most precarious, narrow bit of land with her hand in his, as close to as sea as you could get without a boat, and yet thoroughly anchored. Of building the tree house with her, and how she could make a box into a room, a hidey-hole into a hideaway, a space into a stage. A house into a home.

The darkness and grief and guilt began to lift, just a little. The way a morning mist starts to hint at the brightening sky above before it's gone completely.

"She remembers for you. When you forget," Clara said.

Startled, he drew back. "What do you mean?"

"When I forget my lunch. When I forget my homework. She helps me remember."

You used literally those exact words.

Yeah, you were mad at her the first time, too. At least you're consistent.

Do you want me to tell you what you did? Or what I think you wish you did?

She'd remembered for him, too. And even though it had been hard, she'd put the world back together for him.

"She knows the right things to say to make you feel better."

Shh. Shh, Hunter. It's okay.

That night, dreaming, he'd been in the dark, but he hadn't been alone. He'd wandered through the maze of his own thoughts and followed her voice out again.

It wasn't your fault, Hunter. You did the very best you could.

Trina had been incredibly brave, risking her heart for him twice over. Following him into the dark, holding his hand against the sheer, howling loneliness.

He felt a rush of emotion, gratitude, relief, *love,* sweeping through like sunlight streaming through the mist, like a sudden flood of light, a door opening into a black room, stones falling away from the dank closeness of something caved-in and ominous, washing away the darkness. And in the brief, brilliant illumination, he saw, in the strange familiar frame of memory, his fingers drawing back a strand of Trina's hair, his thumb brushing over her lower lip. He heard his own voice, a slight echo like too much reverb, the sound in his own head.

He remembered. One moment. One sentence. But it was enough.

I know my feelings, and they're not going to change.

26

"Oh, *God,*" Hunter said, his arms dropping to his sides.

"Daddy?" Clara's voice chimed alarm, and she clutched for his hands. "Are you okay?" And then, when he didn't—couldn't—answer right away, "Daddy, are you okay?"

"He's okay, hon. Just a little freaked out."

Nate was standing in the doorway, silhouetted there. Hunter had no idea how long he'd been there. Until he remembered the sharp intake of breath he'd heard when Clara had revealed the nature of her and Phoebe's plot to lure Trina back. So he'd heard the whole conversation.

"Clara, honey," Nate said. "Go on out to Jake and Griff. I want to talk to your dad for a minute."

It took a while before Clara would relinquish her grip on Hunter's hands. He gave her one more kiss on the head and she ran out of the toolshed.

Nate came in and the two men stood there in the semi-darkness. Hunter couldn't even see Nate's face, and that was fine.

"Trina's gone," Hunter said.

"I gathered," said Nate dryly.

"It's my fault. I let her go."

"I know something about that."

Hunter expected him to say more, but Nate stayed quiet, and Hunter was grateful, because it allowed him to gather the frayed scraps of his thoughts into something vaguely coherent.

"The day I lost my memory, there was a woman, trapped, and I flipped out—because that's how Dee died. I'd been trying not to feel anything about her for so long, and then all of a sudden, it was all there. Everything. What I'd taken from her, how much I blamed myself. Not for not saving her, but for not loving her enough."

Nate laughed, then. A short laugh, full of sympathy and amusement. "That's not a thing you get to choose, Hunter. I of all people should fucking know. You don't get to choose who or how much. It chooses you. Actually, it runs you over like a fucking steamroller."

Hunter thought of Trina, furious under the tree-house tree, raging at him. *Don't fucking tell me that, Hunter. Don't tell me you can't do it. Don't tell me what you can and can't give. I've seen you. I know you. And you fell in love with me. So if you're not feeling it now, it's not because you can't. It's because you* won't.

She'd been right, of course. About that. About everything.

Hunter. Those things weren't in your control. That woman's death. Dee's death. How much you love someone.

"I couldn't have saved Dee. Even if I'd loved her enough."

Nate made a gruff, startled noise. "Of course you couldn't."

"And I couldn't have saved that woman."

Nate shook his head. "No."

"My men knew I couldn't. They all knew it was futile. They were telling me to stop. They were telling me to get out before—"

He touched the spot where his chest had been torn open. Where air had rushed out. Where his life had almost fled. But somehow he'd been given it back. Air. Life. The ability to breathe and live and *choose*.

The toolshed no longer seemed so dark. Light filtered through the partially open door and he could see Nate's face clearly now, listening quietly, sympathetically. And he couldn't stop gulping air, any more than he could stop feeling the press of guilt, the crush of grief, the overwhelming sense of anger at how goddamn unfair life could be, but underneath it all the swell of *relief*. Full breaths, his chest rising, air bright and clear and dust-free.

"It's hard to be the one who survives." Nate said it in an almost offhand manner. "You're supposed to be grateful to be alive, but that doesn't mean you are, and it sure as fuck doesn't mean it's easy."

"You mean J.J.?" J.J. had been Nate's best buddy, until he got blown up in the watchtower by an RPG. And that RPG had ended Nate's fight, too, for different reasons.

"'Course I fucking mean J.J.," Nate said. "And you can't look the fact of it, your survival, the other person's death, straight in the face, which makes it a thousand times worse, so it skulks around in your peripheral vision until something finally brings it into focus—"

"Like memory," Hunter said.

And then he stopped for a moment, run over by memories. Not the lost ones, but the new ones. Trina in the airport, expectant and worried, the look on her face when he'd told her he didn't remember, the feel of her mouth on his in the dark, something guiding him back toward the world of the living.

"Like love." Hunter's voice broke.

Eggs over hard, sand and scars, candlelight and chocolate, granola, kissing and kissing and kissing, and the feel of knowing her even though he didn't.

"Like love," Nate agreed, smiling.

Something was gathering in Hunter's gut. Certainty. Resolve. "You said you don't get to choose who you love. And I agree. I know that's true. But you do—"

He took another of those deep breaths, and his ribs protested only the tiniest bit. "You do get to choose what you do about it."

Nate cocked his head to the side. "And what are you going to do about it?"

In answer, Hunter reached into his pocket and pulled out the object he'd found on the closet shelf. A small, black velvet box. It could have contained earrings, but Hunter knew— deeper than memory—that it didn't.

He opened the box. The ring, a single bright glitter of almost-but-not-quite forgotten faith, was unfamiliar, but the tightening of his chest with fear and excitement felt like an echo.

"I found it when I was looking for Clara. I must have bought it, before, and hidden it. It turns out I already knew I wanted to marry her."

"Yeah," said Nate. If Hunter didn't know him better, he would have said his friend's eyes were shiny. "Don't think there was ever much question along those lines, other than how long it would take you to figure it out. Nice ring, by the way."

It was beautiful. A very wise man had obviously picked it out. Hunter was grateful to his previous self. He could get to be friends with that guy, given a little more time.

A chuckle from Nate recalled Hunter to himself and the jewelry balanced on his outstretched hand.

"You shouldn't have. I like you a lot, but I just don't have those kinds of feelings for you."

Hunter raised his head to find Nate grinning at him.

"Go," Nate said, with a dismissive wave of his hand. "Get the fuck to the airport."

27

Phoebe reached over and grabbed Trina's wrist for perhaps the tenth time, consulted the clock on her neglected fitness watch, and sank back into her departure gate seat.

"It's five minutes later than it was the last time you checked," Trina said.

"I'm bored."

"I'm sorry."

"I hate it when you say that. Like it's your fault."

"I'm not saying it because I feel like it's my fault. I'm saying it because I feel sorry. Sympathetic."

"It *is* your fault, though," Phoebe muttered.

Trina shifted uncomfortably in her hard vinyl chair. They'd been sitting at the gate for almost an hour, reading and taking turns playing solitaire and Sudoku and Angry Birds on Trina's phone. And they still had time to kill.

Trina felt suddenly sick of it. The waiting. Not so much the interval until their flight took off, but all the time stretching beyond that into the future. Waiting for the grief and pain to subside. Waiting to be ready to care again. Waiting to feel like her real life wasn't the thing she'd left behind.

She stood abruptly. "You know what?" she said. "I think it's time for retail therapy."

"What's that?" Phoebe asked.

"That's where you spend money you don't have in the vain hope that you'll feel better afterward," Trina said.

A small smile crept over Phoebe's tragic face. "Okay. That sounds kind of fun."

They went out into the central concourse and Trina laid out the rules. "We have thirty-five dollars each. We have to spend almost all of it, but we can't spend more. We can give money to each other, if someone wants to spend more and someone wants to spend less, but we can't spend more than seventy dollars combined. And no one's allowed to buy anything until we visit all the shops."

"Why not?"

"Well, partly so we don't have buyer's remorse," Trina said. "But mainly because window shopping is really the best part, and these rules drag out the window shopping as long as possible. Once you actually spend the money, the retail therapy doesn't work as well."

It was a surprisingly delightful game. They picked things up and put them down—jars of berry jam, packages of smoked salmon, Mariners gear, Seahawks gear, Sounders gear, Storm gear. Cell phone cases, umbrellas, lightweight jackets, laptop satchels, tote bags with the Space Needle emblazoned across their canvas. Books, magazines, packs of gum, Fran's chocolates, snow globes, rain globes, earbuds, trail mix, magnets.

When they'd touched everything there was to touch and grown bored with the hunt, Phoebe spent all her money on books. "Dystopian YA," she said, stroking a glossy paperback image of a dying city and a tough teenaged girl. She borrowed forty-one cents from Trina to make things come out even.

Trina bought a T-shirt with a silkscreen of MoPOP's strange, lumpy architecture, the monorail arcing overhead and through. "I never went to MoPOP," she said. "I've lived in or near Seattle for years, and I never went to MoPOP."

She felt a wave of dizzying grief at that. Misplaced, she knew, but it was as close as she could get to her knotted-up emotions. It was impossible, right now, to think of Hunter or Clara at all. She couldn't even peek at them out of the corner of her mind.

"We need chocolate," she declared.

They bought a giant assortment, sat at a table in the food court, and ate the whole thing.

"So," said Hunter. "You and Phoebe had a plot, huh?"

Clara nodded.

"That was—clever."

"Are you angry?"

He thought about it. "A little," he said. "Because it was sneaky. And it's wrong to trick your parents. And you scared me half to death."

"I'm sorry," she said, starting to cry again.

"But I'm also proud of you," he said. "And grateful to you.

Because you made me think about some things that I didn't want to face up to."

Her tears stopped and her face shone, and he felt just what he'd said: pride and gratitude. And hope.

"The thing about really complicated plots," said Hunter, "is that they don't always work."

She nodded. "I know."

"Because you can set everything up just right, but people don't always do what you think they're going to do. Like I didn't call Trina. I was supposed to call Trina, huh?"

More nodding. "And she would come. And then she'd stay."

He didn't stop to dwell too long on Clara's words. On Clara's complete certainty, despite everything that had happened, that the only obstacle between him and Trina and happiness was his own stubbornness.

He prayed it was the truth.

"It's called the Law of Unintended Consequences, when things happen you didn't predict at all," Hunter said. "Unfortunately, it's more the rule than the exception. The more complicated the plan, the more likely something won't happen exactly the way you think it will."

He looked fondly down at his only child, at her fluffy red hair, her smattering of freckles, her still pug nose. "Do you understand?"

She nodded.

"You can only control your own actions," Hunter said. "That said, for whatever reason, people are absurdly hopeful and keep making plans, and I think that's very brave. And I'd rather be someone who made a plan and tried his best and had it not quite work out than someone who never bothered to make a plan at all because it might not work out the way he hoped."

"Me, too," said Clara fiercely.

"So," he said. "Are you up to try one more?"

"One more what?"

"One more plan."

"Yes!"

He looked at her beautiful, shining face, gazed into the depth of her eyes—so much like Dee's—and prayed he wouldn't disappoint her again.

28

Whed back toward the gate. They'd only taken a few steps, though, before Phoebe reached for Trina's wrist.

"We have a few minutes before boarding," Trina reassured her.

They were a couple hundred feet from the gate when Phoebe asked, "Should you check your phone?"

"For flight alerts? We'll be at the gate in a few seconds. Look—you can see people starting to line up. I bet they just called the back rows."

"Just in case. Before we get on the flight. Shouldn't you check it?"

"I would have felt it buzzing if anyone had called or texted." But she obligingly pulled it out. "Nope," she said. "Nothing."

Phoebe's face darkened.

"Who were you expecting?" Trina inquired carefully.

"No one."

The squirrelly look on Phoebe's face said just the opposite, though.

"Phoebs."

"Now boarding passengers in rows fifteen through twenty-eight."

"That's us," Trina said. "Phoebe, what's going on?"

They joined the amoeba swell of passengers toward the gate door.

"Are you *sure* Hunter didn't call? Or text?"

"To say what?"

"Nothing."

"Phoebe Marie Levine."

Phoebe burst into tears just as they handed their boarding passes to the flight attendant working the gate door.

"Oh, Phoebe," said Trina, awkwardly wrapping one arm around her daughter and maneuvering them up the Jetway side by side. When they stopped, prevented from going any farther by the line in front of them, she wrapped her daughter up, and Phoebe's body shook with sobs.

"She didn't *do* it," Phoebe sobbed.

"Who didn't do what, baby?"

"Clara was going to go *missing,*" Phoebe sobbed. "And Hunter was going to have to call you and make you come home to look for her."

"What?"

"We thought—"

"No, no, I get it," Trina said. "I get it. Oh, sweetheart. Did you really think that would change everything?"

"You told Clara if she needed you, you'd come," Phoebe wept.

"And I meant it," Trina said, her heart squeezing painfully.

"So I thought—"

"But did you really think Hunter would call me?"

"Grandma said he *would,*" Phoebe blurted out.

Ohhhhh.

"Grandma, huh?" Trina said wryly. When had Phoebe started calling Hunter's mom Grandma? "How did she get in on this?"

"She said you guys still loved each other," Phoebe said. "She said she could tell. She said we just had to remind you guys of it, and it would work out."

Half of Trina wanted to tear Linda limb from limb, for stringing the girls along and preying on their emotions like this. And the other half of her wanted to laugh out loud. Good old Linda the Warrior Princess. You could count on her not to give up the fight.

The line in front of them moved forward, and they stepped into the airplane, greeted the first mate and the flight attendant who hovered in the front section, and found their seats. Aisle and center. Trina took the center seat and stowed her carry-on under the seat in front of her.

"Make sure you take your water bottle out of your backpack and put it in your seat-back pocket," she instructed Phoebe. "It'll leak if it's lying down."

She still hadn't addressed what Phoebe had said about how Linda had told the girls that Trina and Hunter still loved each other. She wanted to chicken out, but if the last few weeks had taught her anything, it was the need to do the right thing by her daughter.

She took a deep breath. "I still love Hunter," she said. "He just doesn't love me."

She'd spoken too soon; Phoebe was still hunched over, wedging her water bottle out of her pack. Phoebe surfaced from between her knees and gave her mother a suspicious squinty-eyed look.

"Or, well, he doesn't *think* he loves me."

And suddenly Trina was *mad*. At herself.

"Because he's terrified," she said aloud.

"Mom?"

"He's always *losing* people," she said. "He's terrified of losing people. Of course he pushed us away. And I'm so used to being pushed away, I just said, 'Okay, *sure,* I'll leave before anyone here gets hurt, just show me the door.'"

She would have smacked herself in the head, if gestures like that actually existed.

"Mom?"

Phoebe was clutching something in her hand.

"Someone left something in my seat-back pocket."

She held it out to her mother.

"Oh, Jesus," said Trina.

In the palm of Phoebe's hand lay a small, black velvet box.

She reached for the flight attendant call button, because whoever had lost whatever piece of jewelry was nestled in that box was going to be pretty damn sad about it.

Someone caught her raised wrist from behind.

"Wait," the someone said.

The someone's voice was familiar. Deep, warm, a little husky.

The hand on her wrist was familiar, too. Would be

familiar to her in the darkest room in the darkest moment, if it reached for her.

"It's for you," said another voice, from lower down. A smaller, higher-pitched voice.

"Oh my God, oh my God, oh my God!" said Phoebe, jumping up and down.

Trina turned slowly and found Hunter smiling at her, and she lost her footing and ended up half kneeling on her seat, the velvet box clutched in one hand, Hunter's hand clutched in the other. He pulled her back upright and drew her as close as the seats would allow.

Kiss me, she thought, but he didn't. He just looked into her eyes, and his were dark and full of wishes.

"We're going with you," Clara said brightly.

"You're—"

"I should never have let you leave," Hunter said. "After—" He stopped. "Phoebe. Do you mind if I switch seats with you?"

Phoebe, who looked like she might burst from joy, just nodded, and he traded places with her and sat beside Trina. There was still no one in the window seat beside her.

"After Dee died," he said quietly, "I pushed everything I felt down. I couldn't—I couldn't bear to think of what Dee had lost. Or what Clara had lost."

"Or what *you'd* lost. You lost something, too," Trina said, because she knew he wouldn't say it, out of deference to her. But there was room between them for this piece of history, for all its complexity. There had to be, because he would never be at peace until he owned it. "Maybe you didn't love her as much as anyone can love another person, but you did love her. If you didn't, it wouldn't have broken your heart so much that you couldn't give her what you thought she needed."

He closed his eyes and lifted his hand to his forehead, but she pushed his hand away and leaned close to kiss him where it hurt, instead. And then she made a very, very small sound of satisfaction as his mouth found hers. Just briefly.

He drew back. His eyes shone with affection and gratitude. And maybe—?

She didn't dare hope again. Not quite yet.

"Yes. What I'd lost, too. I pushed it all down and it was back there in the bottom of my brain, and it ambushed me when I saw that other woman in the rubble. It ambushed me then, and the other night when it came back to me in that dream, and it was so much, too much, I couldn't for a little bit see around it to you. But then—then Clara went missing. The girls—"

"Phoebe told me."

"She scared me so bad, Trina. She shook something loose, and for the first time, I let myself—grieve, I guess. And I realized. There are so many things I can't change. Can't fix. But there are so many things I can, things I can make right. People I can treasure and protect—"

The way he was looking at her was making something ache in the very center of her chest, and tears brimmed.

"I promised you that I knew you, that my feelings wouldn't change—"

She stared at him, astonished.

"You remember?"

"After I found Clara and—everything—"

Whatever he was trying to say, he couldn't go any farther. He closed his eyes, opened them again, and smiled at her almost sheepishly. "That's it, though. That's the only thing I remember."

"That's a *lot*," she said.

"Yes. It is a lot. And, Trina—"

He took both her hands in his. "My feelings haven't changed. They never really did. Only how hard I tried not to feel them."

"Oh," she said, because it was all she could manage without crying.

"I tried really damn hard," he said. "But apparently that's not one of the things I have control over. Luckily. Anyway, I'm done trying not to love you."

"I appreciate that," she said dryly, the humor making it possible for her not to begin bawling like a baby. She was uber grateful that there was still no one in that third seat. She could concentrate only on him, his angled, beautiful face, his dark eyes, darker still with love and desire.

"Or—let me put that differently. I love you. I love you so much, Trina."

Her lips parted, but before she could speak, he gestured at the small velvet box. "Open it."

She opened it.

Nestled in the white satin lining lay a ring. The strands of white gold were intertwined like branches, and settled into the middle, like a tree house cradled in the canopy, was a diamond.

"I found it. When I was looking for Clara. It was in my closet. I must have bought it before I deployed."

Her breath caught, hard, in her throat.

"You know what that means. I was going to propose when I came home. I knew. Even then. But now—"

The expression on his face was so open it hurt, like looking into the sun.

"Now I know in all the ways it's possible to know. In my head, but also in my heart. And with every cell in my body. You're funny and strong and smart and you're an amazing mother and you're sexy, not just in an in-bed way, but the whole way you are. No-nonsense and all-in. And you move into a room or a house or a life and make it beautiful, until it's the best place to be in the world."

During that speech, the ache in her chest had turned to warmth and spread to her belly, into her core, radiating out like sun rays even to her fingers and toes.

"And if I forgot a million times and had to start over and over again, I know those are the things I would love about you every time."

In the center of her chest, something blossomed, not a slow unfurling but something brighter and harder. She understood why so many writers, so many literary traditions, located love in the heart. It was hard not to believe it lived there, in the ache and bloom behind her ribs.

"I love you, and I want to spend the rest of my life with you. And if it has to be in L.A. for Phoebe's sake, or because of your job, I totally get it. I don't want to take either of you away from what you need. But just in case it doesn't *have* to be L.A., I did buy us four return-trip tickets."

He pulled a folded envelope from his back pocket and handed it to her.

She was crying, because the ring was so beautiful and he was sliding it onto her finger and the tickets lay on the seat between them, which meant she could go *home* to where she belonged. In his house, in his bed, with her *family*.

"Yes," she said.

His face lit. His eyes, his smile, and something behind it all, a peace she hadn't seen since *before*.

"It doesn't have to be L.A.," she said. "Stefan Spencer has survived twelve years of rarely seeing his daughter. He will learn to live with having a long-distance relationship with her. And the job—" She shrugged. "Sometimes you cling to the past because you can't see the future clearly. I can find a way to do design here just as well as there. Once upon a time it seemed like I needed the glamour of television, but—" She smiled at him. "That feels like a different person, now."

He grinned.

"Whew," he said. "Because I don't think there's much of a market for tree houses in L.A."

HE HAD NEVER SEEN anything quite as beautiful as the bright glow in Trina's face as she looked from the ring to him and back again. Or felt such a deep sense of certainty.

"Do you like it?"

"I love it."

An announcement cut through her words. "If you would please give your attention to the flight attendants—"

"Couldn't have cut it any closer, really, could you?" she asked.

"I could have done a dramatic show-up-in-L.A.-and-beg thing."

"That would have been cool."

"But honestly, I am totally opposed to not having you in my bed tonight."

He settled a kiss against her cheek, near her ear, his breath brushing softly over her skin.

"Mmm." She cast a look over her shoulder. "We don't have a seat mate."

As if on cue, a skinny middle-aged woman with a pinched face made her way up the aisle, maneuvering around the flight attendants doing the safety demonstration. Hunter's blood flow, which had been working its way south in response to the coy look Trina had given him a moment earlier, had to divert back to his brain.

"Spoke too soon," Trina sighed.

They made way for their third seat mate, who was giving off the vibes of the profoundly overwound, muttering about the chain of complicated events that had made her so late. She'd barely gotten her seatbelt fastened when the plane lurched and pulled back from the gate.

"Hey," Trina murmured. "This isn't all on you, you know. What happened. You said you should never have let me leave, but I should never have left. I didn't realize that there was this little voice in my head saying, 'Fine, you don't want us? We don't want you, either.' I guess it's been saying that ever since —ever since Stefan told me he didn't want to help raise Phoebe. And it's made me more defensive on my own and Phoebe's account than I needed to be. You did an awesome job getting by those defenses the first time around, and I just didn't see that you didn't have the resources this time to put up the big fight. Which is *fine*. You don't have to fight anymore, Hunter. You can be done. You can rest. I'll fight for us for a while, until you get your energy back. Okay?"

He felt a swift, glorious sense of relief, as if something infinitely heavy had been lifted off his shoulders. He hadn't realized how *tired* he was. Ever since he'd come to with his head and chest hurting, he'd been exhausted, and even though all along she'd been telling him with her body that he was safe, that he could sleep, he could dream in peace, it meant so much to hear the words coming out of her mouth.

He could rest.

"I love you."

"I love you, too," she said. "And that feels so familiar and so new at the same time. My mother used to say—she and my father had been married thirty years, and she was this weird combination of romantic and pragmatic about it. And she said that the trick is to give yourselves new opportunities all the time. To fall in love again. And that if you can do that, it'll last. So you fall out, because that's the nature of life, that things get stale and time wears you down. But if you're lucky, love renews itself. I guess this gives me faith that no matter what happens to us, we'll fall back in."

He grabbed the back of her head and kissed her full on the mouth, and she didn't hesitate before opening completely to him. She was so warm and soft and giving and—

Their third passenger resettled irritably in her window seat. Hunter released Trina and shifted uncomfortably, his jeans suddenly way too tight.

It was going to be a long flight.

29

"You're in big trouble, obviously."

Phoebe scuffed her sandal on the rug in the airport.

"Both of you," Trina qualified. "You scared years off Hunter's life. And Nate and Jake and Griff's, too. You would have given me a heart attack, had I actually known what was going on."

"He was *supposed* to tell you," Clara said. "That was the whole point."

Clara's face showed defiance, and something occurred, suddenly, to Trina. She crossed her arms and stared Clara down. "You didn't really get your period."

Clara shook her head.

"You lied to me. To get me to stay longer. Yeesh." Trina shook her head. "This is what we get for enrolling them in theater programs," she said to Hunter. "Actresses."

"I'm thinking no more theater *ever*," Hunter said darkly.

"Or softball, for that matter," Trina said.

She was enjoying herself. They sounded like allies. Like *parents.*

They sounded like a *family.*

She snuck a look at him, and he was sneaking a look back. And his eyes held all sorts of emotions, so many she didn't trust herself, suddenly, not to cry.

She didn't even have words for it, for how she'd come back to life. Breathing for what felt like the first time in days. The numbness she hadn't realized had taken over her own body thawing. Her heart beating, hard. Joy like an invader in her veins.

And the look on his face when she'd said yes. He'd lit up, all the blankness gone, a sudden vivid longing painted all over him.

This was everything she'd never dared hope for.

Her silence must have scared the hell out of the children because Clara suddenly burst out with, "It was Grandma's idea!" like she'd cracked under intensive interrogation.

"You hiding, you mean?" Hunter said.

"Not just the hiding," said Clara, very, very quietly.

Trina and Hunter both turned on her, and Hunter demanded, "Do you mean it was Grandma's idea to pretend you had your period?"

The last word came out like Hunter wasn't quite sure of it.

He'd never have been able to deal with menstruation without me, Trina thought. And hid her smile so the kids wouldn't see.

"You've been—plotting with Grandma all along? What, like on the phone?" Hunter sounded incredulous.

Both girls were nodding.

"You, too?" Trina asked Phoebe.

More nodding.

Trina finally gave up on pretending she wasn't impressed. "Wow."

"I'm going to kill her," Hunter said.

"Don't kill Grandma!" both girls said simultaneously.

"We'll figure out some suitable consequences for all *three* of you," Trina said.

"Grandma is grounded for a year. No phone privileges till she's ninety," Hunter growled. But she could see he was wrestling a smile, too. It made her heart feel two sizes too big.

It made her want to cave in every possible way, which in turn made her stand up straighter and put more steel in her spine as she addressed the girls. "You know this is very serious." But she, too, was having trouble with the corners of her mouth. "You lied to us. Outright. You deceived us and scared us and—"

"But it *worked*!" cried Clara. "You're going to *stay*!"

Suddenly Trina's chest felt terribly, terribly tight and she had to blink, hard.

"Oh, honey," Trina said. And put her arms around both girls. She snuck a look at Hunter, who nodded. "Yes. Phoebe and I are staying."

One of the girls in her arms gave a shriek of delight, and then both of them were talking at once. "We thought you were!" "Phoebe said you were!" "It's pretty cool that he followed you to the airport. It's really romantic." "Not that we like romance. We think it's gross. But still." "Does this mean you're getting *married*?"

"Yes."

There was an interval of loud hooting and hollering and quiet, tearful hugging.

"And then he'll be my father? And you'll be her mother? And we'll be *sisters*?"

Phoebe's tone was so reverent that it made Trina's breath catch.

"He'd be your stepfather. And I'd be Clara's stepmother. And you'd be stepsisters."

"But good stepsisters. Not evil stepsisters."

"Speaking of which," Trina said. "You're still in trouble. No electronic devices for three days. Including all telephones."

It was testament to the happiness of the moment that Clara and Phoebe barely even groaned.

30

"Shh."

She woke to find a hand over her mouth, and she bit it, hard. The owner of the hand grunted and resolved into Hunter.

"You were making a lot of noise."

"Because your hand is in my pants," she pointed out. The other one was hot against the crotch of her flimsy panties, which were now *wet* flimsy panties.

"You liked it. You were rocking against it."

She wasn't going to argue about that. She could feel how swollen she was and wondered how long she'd been moving against him, but she put that question out of her head and resumed the rhythm she'd left off.

"You fell asleep waiting for me to finish putting the girls to bed," he whispered. They were staying in two adjoining rooms at a hotel near the airport.

"Sorry," she whispered back. Only she wasn't. Not anymore. Hard to be sorry about anything when he'd found exactly the right spot to rest his palm against her. *Ungh.*

But it wasn't quite enough. Not the pressure against her body, not his other hand idly swirling near her nipple. She arched her back to try to get more of both, but he failed to oblige. He was doing it on purpose, the bastard, teasing her. She moaned and closed her thighs around his hand.

"Tell me a story?"

She smiled into the dark.

"Was it good, even the first time? Was I nervous? I bet I desperately wanted to completely and totally snow you. Ruin you for all men for all time. That's how I felt the first time in the tree house."

"I don't think so. If you were, you sure as hell didn't show it—either time. You were super in charge, super alpha. Sexy." Her whole body flushed, remembering the power of *his* body over and in her.

"Make that sound again."

"Which one?"

"The one you just made."

"I didn't."

"You did. Like a breath and a moan. Were you thinking about it?"

"Yeah."

"About me *fucking* you that first time?"

Earlier that evening, while the girls had been reading in the other hotel room before bed, he'd reread all the emails they'd sent back and forth while he was deployed. It wasn't quite as good as getting his memory back, he'd told her, but it came damn close. In one of them, she'd referenced a discussion they'd had about dirty talk, and he'd made her rehash the conversation. It had taken place early in their days together, when he'd sworn aloud during sex, then apologized, and she'd told him she liked the word *fucking,* even used as a verb. She'd told him she liked dirty talk, the way it felt in her own mouth, as if the words had weight and shape, something she could swirl her tongue over. And she liked it in his mouth, the words twining and insinuating, amping her up faster than touch.

Oh, really? he'd said, giving her a look that said the girls' bedtime couldn't come soon enough.

Really, she'd said, smirking.

He slid a finger easily into her, then another. In. Out. A pace just slow enough to make her desperate for more. "Hunter."

"Mmm-hmm?"

"I wanted to spoil you for all women that first night, too. I wanted to blow away your reasons we shouldn't be together. I wanted you to forget all of them."

"There were *no* good reasons we shouldn't."

"Well, except the girls. Being careful of their feelings. That was legit."

"Which we pretty much sucked at."

"Yeah." His thick, strong fingers between her legs were muddling up her thinking. "We tried. Neither of us was counting on amnesia."

"And PTSD."

They both got really quiet then. He didn't remove his fingers from inside her, but his movements stilled.

"You—gonna be okay?" she asked.

He took his hand away and sighed. "Not yet. Not completely. But I'm here. And I think I'll get a little more okay each day, with setbacks. I'll get some help. I've got a therapy referral, and Jake gave me some info about counselors and groups."

"Is that—would you do that? I know guys aren't always into that stuff."

"If it were just me? No. But I've got the girls to think of, and you. So I want to do whatever I can to be okay. And if it means sitting and talking it out with someone, whatever, I can handle it. Sometimes that's what it takes to man up, you know? Doing something that's out of your comfort zone. Plus it does help to talk to other people who've been there. Nate said some stuff to me that really resonated. He said, 'It's hard to be the one who survives. You're supposed to be grateful to be alive, but that doesn't mean you are.'"

His words made her heart hurt. "You feel like that? Like you aren't grateful to be the one who lived?"

"Sometimes."

"Like—you wish it weren't that way?" She was holding her breath.

"You mean would I off myself? No. No fucking way. But does it feel like it's all wrong? Hell yeah."

"When that happens—when you feel like it's all wrong—tell me? And I'll—" She hesitated. "I'll make you forget. Just for a little while. Just as long as you need to, to be glad you're alive."

He rolled her over, his mouth searching hers out in the dark, and when his found it he gave her the most overwhelming sensation of coming home. In the dark, he blew a breath out, and she reached for his hand and held it, hard.

"Would you do that, now?"

His voice was low and a little shaky.

"God, yeah. Any time. Every fucking time."

And she did.

31

She'd expected it to be more . . . prepossessing. It was just an office building with hundreds of small glass windows, surrounded by a not-terribly-elegant fence. She did have to give her name, and Stefan's, at the security station in the front, but the guy in the booth reminded her more of a parking-lot attendant than the kind of high-minded caricature you'd see in the movies or . . . on TV. It was kind of funny that even when TV portrayed TV, it fancied it up.

Stefan stepped out of the elevator, looking—well, good. Movie-star handsome. But her heart didn't skip a beat or clench with longing, and there was no regret left anywhere in her. He was just a man. Maybe if he'd never stood on a stage with that ferocious snake-oil salesman energy, she never would have seen him as anything other than a good friend. But then Phoebe wouldn't have been born, so she couldn't regret even that.

He hugged her, and she let him. And then she said, "I'm so sorry, Stefan."

Startled, he scanned her face thoroughly, but still looked puzzled.

"I can't take the job. I can't stay. We're not going to stay."

"What do you mean, you're not going to stay?"

"I'm sorry about the bait and switch. I know you held the job for me—"

"Damn straight I held the job for you."

"But I also know there are probably a hundred people breathlessly waiting behind me, and that it's going to take you all of ten minutes to fill it."

A little flicker in his expression acknowledged the truth of that. But he shook his head. "I don't understand."

"Can we go somewhere we can talk?"

He took her to the cafeteria and they sat and drank bad coffee while she told him the story. The whole story, including his unintended role in it.

"I see," he said, when she was done.

"Do you?"

He was no longer angry. His face had sagged a little, and she could see how he'd look when he got older. She was reminded about how brutal his profession was, how unforgiving. Behind the glamour, that was the truth of it.

The creases in Stefan's brow deepened. "He's like the anti-me, right? He stuck it out with his pregnant girlfriend and kid. He stayed because it was the right thing to do. And I left. I abandoned the two of you, even knowing it was the wrong thing to do."

She didn't know what to say. Whether to argue with him, say that *wrong* was a strong word, that she and Phoebe had been okay. Or—to let him own his failure.

"From what you've told me, Hunter is the kind of father Phoebe deserves to have."

There, she wouldn't argue.

He took a deep breath. "I'd hoped for a second chance with Phoebe. But there just aren't that many second chances in life. I can't blame you at all for wanting to grab hold of yours. But you'll let her visit?"

"Of course," she said. "I do want her to know you. And get to spend time with you. She's getting old enough that she could probably fly down here on her own occasionally. Weekends here and there. You'd buy her ticket, of course." She didn't even bother to feel guilty about that. Stefan could afford it, and there was that whole matter of back child support . . .

"Absolutely," Stefan said.

Maybe he would and maybe he wouldn't buy those tickets, and when he disappointed them or canceled at the last minute, that would be okay, too.

She and Hunter would take the girls on a marvelous consolation trip instead.

She sat with Stefan for a while longer, talking about Phoebe, mainly; then he excused himself, saying he had to get back to the office to offer the job she'd just turned down to someone else.

Later that day, he led the four of them on a studio tour, introduced them to his stunning actress girlfriend, and took them out to dinner at his favorite restaurant, pointing out stars to the dazzled girls. But Trina noted that he never asked Phoebe anything about what she liked to do or what was important to her, and by the end of the evening, she could tell from his body language—and his girlfriend's—that both were eager to say goodbye.

Stefan didn't offer to take Phoebe out for lunch or do anything else with her, and in the hotel room afterward, Trina sat with her almost-full-sized daughter curled up in her lap while Phoebe sobbed her hurt out.

"Not everyone is cut out to be a dad," Trina said quietly. And felt grateful that Stefan had known that about himself at age seventeen, long before she'd been willing to accept it about him.

A few minutes later, the tears having subsided to occasional hiccups, Phoebe said, "I'm glad we're not staying here. I'm glad we're going home."

The word *home* cut a warm swath through Trina's chest. The ease with which Phoebe said it.

"Hunter is a good dad. Don't you think?"

That took Trina's breath away. When she could speak again, she said, "Yes. Yes, he is."

"Do you remember when we had the stomach flu?" Phoebe asked.

It had been a while since she'd looked, really looked, at her daughter. There was a smattering of small pimples at the side of Phoebe's nose, and her eyebrows had darkened from baby strawberry blond to a more adult color. Her expression was older than her years.

Funny that she was asking about that night, which had been a turning point for her and Hunter a year ago. "Yeah."

"Hunter held my head the first time I threw up."

Of course he had. It had never occurred to Trina to ask what had happened before she'd arrived at Hunter and Clara's that night, but of course he had.

Her heart filled with love for him. Her heart would always be filled with love for him.

I promised my feelings for you wouldn't change. And, Trina— they never really did. Only how hard I tried not to feel them.

"Hunter is the best man I know," Trina said quietly. "Stefan—he's not perfect, but he'll be a friend to you, if you let him, and that's worth something, for sure. But you can let Hunter be your family. And your home."

Phoebe sighed, the soft, yielding sigh at the end of a good cry, and settled more thoroughly against her mother, and Trina held her tight and felt her heart overflow with gratitude.

THE FOUR OF them drove out to see Linda and Ray, who had a lovely, immaculately kept double-wide in an beautiful park north of L.A. Ray was a short, bald retired Coast Guard admiral who appeared to be a decade younger than Linda; Hunter couldn't bring himself to ask. The introduction between Hunter and Ray was awkward, since Ray had met Hunter once before and Hunter couldn't remember one fucking thing about the guy, but he'd just have to get used to the occasional mental blank along those lines. There were little scraps here and there coming back to him from the past, but he wasn't putting his life on hold to wait for everything to return in a rush. Not gonna happen.

He let his mom take the girls for short motorcycle rides. Trina couldn't even watch; she had to go inside, and afterward she said she'd covered her ears. But both of them agreed that there was a fine line between protecting against risk and depriving kids of experiences, and a few hundred helmeted yards on a Gold Wing on deserted roads with a grandmother at the handlebars was a pretty low-risk proposition.

Afterward, Hunter and Linda went for a walk, and he told her what had happened, the whole story, from Clara's disappearance to the proposal on the airplane.

"Thank *God* you came to your senses," Linda said.

"I heard you played a role."

She ducked her head.

"Mom."

"I might have made a few suggestions here and there."

"Fake her period? Go missing?"

"You're not mad, are you?"

"Of course I'm mad," he said. "You manipulated two little girls to get your way. You manipulated me and Trina. That's not acceptable, and I don't want anything like that to happen again."

She gave him a look. It was the same look she'd given him countless times over the course of his life when he'd broken a rule or come home after curfew or talked back to her. "Someone had to get you to see the light," she said sternly. "And who else, if not your mother?"

They were rounding back on the trailer now, and Ray was showing Clara and Phoebe something in the motorcycle engine, while Trina watched. The expression on her face—

She was glowing. He'd never seen her that happy. And while he watched, she looked down at her hand and turned his ring this way and that, admiring. He almost couldn't stand the rush of love he felt; it seemed to want to knock him off his feet.

"Besides," his mother said, and he looked up to see her watching his family—his *family*—with an expression not unlike Trina's. "You have to admit, it worked. Right?"

He didn't have to answer that, because she looked up then and saw the expression on *his* face, and she said, "Oh, Hunter, that's all I ever wanted for you," and burst into tears.

32

The sun shone brilliantly on Hunter and Trina's mid-September wedding day. Hunter stood beside Nate under the arbor that he'd built and the girls and Trina had threaded with ribbons and greens and flowers. The audience stretched before him—his parents and siblings, Trina's older sisters, Stefan and his girlfriend, Jake and Mira and Sam, Alia with Nate's adopted family Suzy, Jim, and Braden, and a few of his platoon-mates who were back stateside.

The DJ started the wedding march and Phoebe and Clara came down the aisle toward him.

"I know they're too old, but I always wanted flower girls," Trina had said, and so they were dressed in identical white dresses with pale blue sashes, and they scattered rose petals as they walked, looking a little pale and tremulous and deliberately not making eye contact with all the people on either side of them.

They didn't look anything like sisters, Clara with her frothy cloud of bright red hair and Phoebe's all satin blond,

Clara's face freckled and angular, Phoebe's fair and heart-shaped just like Trina's—but as they came close to him they snuck looks at each other and exchanged smiles that tipped up at opposite corners, and it struck him that they were sisters, in their hearts, and probably always had been.

But then he couldn't watch them anymore because Trina had stepped around the side of the house and was coming toward him, and his breath stuck hard in his chest.

Her dress wasn't anything fancy. He didn't know all the official names for fabrics and cuts, but this one was made out of a light-looking fabric, silk, maybe, pure white. It had skinny little straps and an uneven, draped front, and a high waist that made her breasts look even bigger and softer and rounder and—

Wasn't he supposed to be thinking loftier thoughts than this?

He couldn't spend too much time staring at her breasts—he could indulge in that later, anyway—because as soon as she was close enough for him to see her face, he couldn't look anywhere else. She was wearing just a little bit of makeup and smiling a sweet, small, secret smile, and she *glowed*. And her eyes were on his and her smile grew *for him* and he thought his heart was absolutely going to burst.

I've never felt like this before, he wanted to say. *I've never felt anything remotely like this, ever before.*

He tried to tell her with his eyes, and maybe he succeeded, just a little, because as she got closer he could see that her eyes were full of tears, the way they'd been on the airplane when he'd told her how he felt. He'd always thought it was just crazy talk when people said they had eyes only for one another, but he swore to God it was like there was no one else in the backyard. And in fact, everyone around them had fallen silent, probably because they all wanted to stare at her, too, at her beautiful hair piled up on her head and the diamonds sparkling in her earlobes and in the hollow of her throat.

She'd refused to stay in his house the night before—said that even though they'd been together already it wasn't lucky—and had gone to stay at Bonnie's, and he couldn't believe how fast he'd gotten used to having her in his bed. It felt so big and cold and goddamn empty, and he'd lain sleepless for hours wanting to bury himself in her. He guessed a body could get damn used to frequent sex pretty quickly, and he didn't know if it was how they'd *always* be, but for the last few months it had been twice a day at least—quick in the morning, with the door locked against intruders, and slow and languorous at night.

"Hi," she said, arriving at his side.

It made him laugh. Everything was so formal and serious, and she was just *her*.

"Hey, you."

The justice of the peace began to speak, but he didn't hear it. He only saw the sparkle of her blue eyes and the way that smile softly curved her mouth. He saw her chest rise and fall. He didn't hear another word until it was time for the vows.

Her eyes brimmed with tears, but her voice was steady. "I, Trina . . . take thee, Hunter . . . to be my husband . . . to have and to hold . . . from this day forward . . . for better, for worse . . . for richer, for poorer . . . in sickness and in health . . . to love and to cherish . . . till death do us part."

He felt no qualms. No doubts. No sense of worry that he might not be enough for her or she for him.

Phoebe was crying. Clara unwrapped a handkerchief from somewhere inside her bouquet and handed it over.

And then it was his turn to say his.

"I, Hunter . . . take thee, Trina . . . to be my wife . . . to have and to hold . . . from this day forward . . . for better, for worse . . . for richer, for poorer . . . in sickness and in health . . ."

He hesitated.

It wasn't enough. Not *quite.*

"In light and in darkness," he said.

Someone in the audience gasped. Trina looked up at him, startled.

"In memory and in forgetting."

"Hunter."

"I just wanted you to know," he whispered. "In case I get old and senile. My body doesn't forget. My heart doesn't forget."

They were off script and she was off balance, a little wild-eyed, and he reached out to steady her. "To love and to cherish," he said, smiling. "Till death do us part."

"By the power vested in me by the state of Washington, I now pronounce you husband and wife," the JP said. "You may kiss the bride."

He did, brushing her tears away and whispering to her that it was okay, everything was okay, they were going to be just fine.

EPILOGUE

Jake and Mira usually held their annual picnic in their big backyard, but this year, they held it at R&R in honor of the completion of the veterans' retreat's newest wing, a series of tree houses constructed by Hunter and Trina.

"Hey, man. You enjoying life out of the army?" said Nate, coming up beside them.

Hunter grinned at him. "I don't miss it, I'll tell you that."

Nate got serious for a moment. "I do. Sometimes. Just— the camaraderie, you know? Although—" He laughed. "I know if I want someone to swear at me and kick my ass, there's always Jake. Speaking of which, you want to head out with us on our next trip?"

"Sure." Hunter's casual shrug masked real pleasure.

"The tree houses are *amazing*," Nate said, gesturing skyward.

"Thanks," Hunter and Trina said together.

"Do you two do other work besides tree houses?" Alia asked, smiling at Trina. "Nate and I just bought a house nearby, and I'd love to have you do built-ins and decorate our living room. It's *meh* right now, and just looking at what you did up there gave me a million ideas."

"I haven't, but—sure. I'd love to."

"All the little details. The wraparound deck, the built-in bunks—and the grain in some of that wood, too."

"In that one?" Hunter pointed. "That's quarter-sawn oak. You wouldn't believe how hard it is to get quarter-sawn oak of that quality. There's basically one guy in the U.S. who takes that kind of care with cutting for the beauty of the grain."

"Well, it's worth it."

The tree houses at R&R were their second joint project. They were intended for veterans who wanted to visit the retreat with their wives and children instead of alone. They'd been built by a small crew under the direction of Hunter, and decorated by Trina, with help from her own crew of Phoebe and Clara.

A week before, they'd celebrated a similar success several hundred miles north—the opening of a bed-and-breakfast in a series of tree houses they'd been commissioned to build. They'd walked away from the event with several business cards in their pockets.

But there was something special about the project at R&R. Maybe the enthusiasm of the vets themselves, who were like little boys as they explored the tree houses' features —circular staircases, wood-and-rope suspension bridges, wraparound decks, bunks and lofts, and a bajillion built-ins.

Trina had interviewed veterans' families for hours, asking what they needed in order to feel comfortable. There were quiet curtained-off areas that were simple, nearly bare, where the vets could retreat from their thoughts and the clutter of the world. Secret corners where kids could hide and seek. Nooks that soothed spouses who'd been frayed and frazzled by the borrowed stresses of their partners. And views of the outside to call them all out of hiding and back into the world and nature—a peek here at the beach and the lake; a tiny wedge of the archery range; a path, wandering away into the woods and beckoning visitors to follow.

But if Hunter hadn't built her such inspiring places, such perfect cocoons high up in the world, she wouldn't have had half the pleasure in putting her stamp on them.

"We love working together," she said, smiling at Hunter.

He gave her back a smile that was 80 percent public and 20 percent private, and that was enough to make her face heat up.

"Ah," said Nate. "The romance of a Jake-and-Mira picnic. Did I ever tell you two lovebirds that Alia and I met at one of these?"

"Really?"

"Uh-huh," said Alia. She was a pretty, athletic woman with dark hair, freckles, and a totally infectious smile. They'd met once before—with Nate and Hunter—though Hunter still had no memory of that episode. Earlier today, Trina had hung out with Mira and Alia, and the three women had hit it off. "I thought he was interested in my sister, but it turned out —one very messy love triangle later—"

"That I had eyes only for her," Nate said, grinning at her.

"Speaking of romance at Jake and Mira's picnics . . ." Nate tilted his head and they all looked toward the clearing where there was a Wiffle ball game in progress. Well, more or less in progress. At the moment, Clara was chasing Braden, trying to tag him with a Wiffle ball even though they were *nowhere* near the base path, and Phoebe was wrestling the bat out of Sam's hands. They were all laughing, red-faced and sweaty.

"Young love," Nate intoned.

Hunter frowned. "I am *so* not ready for this."

"Better get yourself ready. As the father of *two girls,* you're going to have to polish up your weapons of war and practice looking threatening."

"Oh, believe me, both those girls can more than take care of themselves," Trina said dryly. Even though Clara and Phoebe had since both gotten their periods, she still hadn't *quite* gotten over that deception—or how much it had tugged on her heart. "It's Sam and Braden I feel sorry for."

And they all watched as the girls booked it for the woods, boys in pursuit.

"Did I hear a rumor . . .?" Trina asked tentatively, and both Nate's and Alia's grins got bigger.

"Yup," said Nate, resting a proprietary hand on Alia's belly. "November."

"Congratulations!"

"Thank you," Alia said.

"We were actually hoping you could build us a tree house. So we can put him out there and get a little bit of sleep." Nate laughed. A little nervously.

"You'll be fine," said Trina. "By the time he's— He?"

They nodded confirmation.

"By the time he's twelve, he'll be sleeping in and you'll start to feel better."

Nate groaned. "That's what I was afraid of."

"If you come visit us at our place," Trina said, "the girls can babysit and the four of us can go out."

"Sounds like a plan to me," Alia said. "Or, we can host

some get-togethers at our place and Jake and Mira and Sam can head our way, too. We have plenty of guest space."

"And Griff. Don't forget Griff," Nate said.

Alia and Nate exchanged looks, and Trina got the feeling there was a whole story there, but she didn't pry. "Of course," she said. "The more the merrier. But gender-separated rooms for the teenagers."

"Amen to that," Nate said. "Also, we'll be doing our best to lure you and Hunter down here permanently. What do you think? Tree house business on the Oregon coast? Sounds like a win to me." He grinned. "All right, Li, dessert's served and it looks incredible. Let's load up. Catch you guys before you take off, okay? We'll make plans."

When they were alone, Trina tipped her head back and looked up at their handiwork. "They're beautiful," she said, resting her head against Hunter's shoulder.

"Thanks to *you*," he said. "Before you got your hands on them, they were merely well-crafted." He dropped a kiss on her hair, and then dipped his head to kiss her just a little longer than was family-friendly.

She didn't mind, despite a few catcalls and whistles and *get a room* exhortations. She was feeling insanely happy. Not just about the man who hadn't left her side for a moment today, but also about the work they'd done together.

Still, it was the story of how the business had come to be in the first place that Trina loved most. In classic style, they'd had the same great idea at the same time. In secret, Trina had contacted Jake and talked him into the idea of building the two new units high in the branches of R&R's beautiful old trees. But she'd made him agree to use Hunter's contracting services and her own design expertise.

At the same time, in secret, Hunter had reached out to a friend of Nate's who wanted to start a B&B that took advantage of some wild and beautiful land he'd purchased in Washington. And Hunter had held out on signing the contract he'd negotiated until the new B&B owner had decided to employ Trina to do the interior work on the new, canopy-hugging rooms.

The best part was that they'd both decided to break their surprises to each other over a candlelit dinner (and chocolate cake dessert) in their own newly finished getaway. Hunter had barely gotten a few words out before Trina was laughing.

"What's so funny?" he demanded. "I think it's a fabulous idea!"

She'd explained.

"Great minds think alike," Hunter had said, and then they'd celebrated the abundance of work by opening a bottle of champagne and licking it off each other's bodies.

"What are you thinking about?" he asked now, brushing a strand of hair behind her ear.

"Why?"

He leaned close. "You just blushed all the way down to your cleavage. And mighty fine cleavage it is, too, I might add."

She told him.

"Mmm," he said.

"It could be a tradition. For celebrating things."

"What sorts of things?"

"All sorts of things."

"The opening of a new wing at a veterans' retreat, for example?"

"That seems like a good thing to celebrate."

His eyes, dark and intent, held hers. "But let's work some things out ahead of time, okay?"

She nodded.

"You tell Jake and Mira we need a separate room for the girls."

"You buy the champagne."

"You wear that sexy blue silk nightgown thing."

"You tell the bedtime story."

She let out a long, slow exhalation, trying not to make it audible to everyone else at the picnic.

"And then we can do what we do best," he said.

"What's that?" she teased.

He dropped a soft kiss on her parted lips, stared into her eyes just long enough to make her toes curl, then leaned down, his breath brushing over her ear to start a chain reaction of sensations swirling through her body.

"Make new memories."

ACKNOWLEDGMENTS

This book—and I—benefitted in its initial publication from the perspective of not only one but two editors at Penguin Random House (Loveswept)—Sue Grimshaw and Sarah Murphy.

To my agent, Emily Sylvan Kim: I have LOVED getting to spend more time with you this year. What a joy to have you visit my neck of the woods! And—of course—thank you for all the help and support you give so generously all the time at every stage of the process. Having you in my corner is a superpower in and of itself.

To my two Ambers: thank you, Amber Shah, for building and repairing my Web site, and Amber Belldene, for building up my ego and repairing my sanity (among other acts of friendship too numerous to name). To Rachel, thank you for the walks, wise words, and open ear. And there are so many other women, too many to name, who give me the strength and courage to do this sometimes very crazy job of ours.

To my Hero, my Girl, and my Boy: You guys are saints and a constant delight and I couldn't do any of this without you. I love you.

Because this book is a re-release, I also have quite a few additional people to thank, people who have been instrumental in helping me get this book back out in the world (and/or in saving my sanity in the process): Karen Booth, Sarina Bowen, Cheryl Cain, Kate Davies, Christine D'Abo (with sugar and post-its on top), Gretchen Douma, Nicole French, Rachel Grant (again and again and again), Molly Hays, Gwen Hayes, Gwen Hernandez, Sierra Hill, Christy Hovland, Kris Kennedy, Claire Kingsley, Jaycee Lee, Kathy McGowan, Alexa Rowan, Ellen Schroer, Jessica Scott (again), Lauren Seilnacht, Sierra Simone, Darya Swingle, Skye Warren, the attendees of Seattle Unconference 2018, the members of Emerald City Author Chicks, the members of Living the Dream Mastermind, and about a bajillion other people. I hope I'm not forgetting anyone, but I might be, because there are so, so many generous authors out there willing to buoy each other up, and everyone I turned to during this process gave their time and support generously.

I also want to thank Melissa McCulloch for her wisdom on design issues—she was abundantly generous with her time and knowledge, and I learned so much from her. Plus, I had a blast doing it—Melissa, I adore you.

Also, extra thanks to the best (and sexiest) tech consultant ever, the inimitable Mr. Bell.

ALSO BY SERENA BELL

Returning Home

Hold On Tight

Can't Hold Back

To Have and to Hold

Holding Out

Tierney Bay

So Close

So True

So Good (2021)

So Right (2022)

Sexy Single Dads

Do Over

Head Over Heels

Sleepover

New York Glitz

Still So Hot!

Hot & Bothered

Standalone

Turn Up the Heat

ABOUT THE AUTHOR

USA Today bestselling author Serena Bell writes contemporary romance with heat, heart, and humor. A former journalist, Serena has always believed that everyone has an amazing story to tell if you listen carefully, and you can often find her scribbling in her tiny garret office, mainlining chocolate and bringing to life the tales in her head.

Serena's books have earned many honors, including an RT Reviewers' Choice Award, Apple Books Best Book of the Month, and Amazon Best Book of the Year for Romance.

When not writing, Serena loves to spend time with her college-sweetheart husband and two hilarious kiddos—all of whom are incredibly tolerant not just of Serena's imaginary friends but also of how often she changes her hobbies and how passionately she embraces the new ones. These days, it's stand-up paddle boarding, board-gaming, meditation, and long walks with good friends.

Made in the USA
Coppell, TX
23 March 2021

52233629R00152